THE FERTILITY OF EVIL

ALSO BY AMARA LAKHOUS

Clash of Civilizations Over an Elevator in Piazza Vittorio

Divorce Islamic Style

Dispute Over a Very Italian Piglet

The Prank of the Good Little Virgin of Via Ormea

THE FERTILITY OF EVIL

AMARA LAKHOUS

Translated from the Arabic by
Alexander E. Elinson

OTHER PRESS | NEW YORK

Originally published in Arabic as *Tair al-lail* in 2019 by
Manshurat Al-Mutawassit

Published by special arrangement with Actes Sud

Production editor: Yvonne E. Cárdenas
Text designer: Patrice Sheridan
This book was set in Minion Pro by
Alpha Design & Composition of Pittsfield, NH

1 3 5 7 9 10 8 6 4 2

 Printed in the United States of America on acid-free paper. For information write to Other Press LLC,
267 Fifth Avenue, 6th Floor, New York, NY 10016.
Or visit our Web site: www.otherpress.com

Library of Congress Cataloging-in-Publication Data
Names: Lakhous, Amara, 1970- author | Elinson, Alexander E. translator
Title: The fertility of evil : a novel / Amara Lakhous ; translated from the Arabic by Alexander E. Elinson.
Other titles: Ṭayr al-layl. English
Description: New York : Other Press, 2026.
Identifiers: LCCN 2025029510 (print) | LCCN 2025029511 (ebook) |
ISBN 9781635425833 paperback | ISBN 9781635425840 ebook
Subjects: LCGFT: Thrillers (Fiction) | Novels | Fiction
Classification: LCC PJ7944.A47 T3913 2026 (print) |
LCC PJ7944.A47 (ebook)
LC record available at https://lccn.loc.gov/2025029510
LC ebook record available at https://lccn.loc.gov/2025029511

Publisher's Note

This is a work of fiction. Names, characters, places, and incidents either are the product of the author's imagination or are used fictitiously, and any resemblance to actual persons, living or dead, events, or locales is entirely coincidental.

Dedicated to

Elaine

and

Mokhtar Mokhtefi

LIST OF CHARACTERS

(IN ALPHABETICAL ORDER)

Abbas Badi, aka Stork—Member of a *fidaï* cell operating in Oran during the Algerian Revolution (1954–62) alongside Zahra Misbah, Miloud Sabri, and Driss Talbi

Zuhour Badi—Abbas Badi's "registered" daughter

General Brahim Belkacemi—Colonel Karim Soltani's superior officer

Badreddine Bouzar, or Badrou—Law student; becomes Miloud Sabri's disciple and Mona Sabri's husband

Amira Derbal—Redouane Derbal's sister and Badrou Bouzar's secretary

Redouane Derbal—Badrou Bouzar's childhood friend; terrorist

First Lieutenant Malika Derraji—Aide to Colonel Karim Soltani in the Anti-Terrorism Unit

Rachid Kadri—Political cartoonist; Souad Sabri's lover

Omar Mansouri—Cousin and superior to Yazid

Yazid Mansouri—Superior officer of Abbas Badi, Zahra Misbah, Miloud Sabri, and Driss Talbi during the Revolution

Meriem, or Meryouma—Colonel Karim Soltani's lover

Farida Misbah—Resistance fighter during the Algerian Revolution; sister of Youssef and Zahra Misbah, wife of Driss Talbi, and mother of Nabil Talbi

Youssef Misbah—Liaison agent for *fidaï* networks in Oran during the war; Military Security officer post-independence, entrepreneur; brother of Farida and Zahra Misbah

Zahra Misbah, aka Dolores—Member of a *fidaï* cell in Oran during the War of Independence alongside Abbas Badi, Miloud Sabri, and Driss Talbi; sister of Farida and Youssef Misbah, wife of Miloud Sabri, and mother of Mona and Souad Sabri

Professeur Pierre Rondeau—History teacher at Ardaillon High School, where Abbas Badi, Miloud Sabri, and Driss Talbi were students

Miloud Sabri, aka Hoopoe—Member of the same *fidaï* cell as Abbas Badi, Zahra Misbah, and Driss Talbi; husband of Zahra Misbah and father of Mona and Souad Sabri

Mona Sabri—Daughter of Zahra Misbah and Miloud Sabri, wife of Badrou Bouzar

Souad Sabri—Daughter of Zahra Misbah and Miloud Sabri, Rachid Kadri's lover

Colonel Karim Soltani—Head of the Anti-Terrorism Unit

Driss Talbi, aka Falcon—Member of the same *fidaï* cell as Abbas Badi, Zahra Misbah, and Miloud Sabri; lawyer and human rights advocate; husband of Farida Misbah and father of Nabil Talbi

Nabil Talbi—Journalist; son of Farida Misbah and Driss Talbi

Captain Samir Ziane—Aide to Colonel Karim Soltani in the Anti-Terrorism Unit

HISTORICAL TIMELINE

July 5, 1830	The French occupy the city of Algiers
June 22, 1834	France formally annexes occupied Algeria as a military-ruled colony
1832–47	Emir Abdelkader leads a rebellion against French colonial rule
1848	Algeria is declared an integral part of France, divided into three administrative units, or *départements* (Algiers, Oran, and Constantine)
July 14, 1865	It is decreed that colonized indigenous inhabitants of Algeria are subject to French laws but are not French citizens
1870	The Crémieux Decree grants Algerian Jews (but not Muslims) French citizenship
Oct. 10, 1954	National Liberation Front is established
1954–62	Algerian War of Independence, or Revolution
July 1, 1962	Referendum on Algerian Independence (passed with 99.72 percent of the vote)

JULY 5, 1962	Algerian Independence Day recognized
1963–65	Ahmed Ben Bella serves as Algeria's first president
JUNE 19, 1965	Houari Boumediene deposes Ahmed Ben Bella in a military coup; Boumediene serves as president until he dies on December 27, 1978
FEB. 9, 1979	Chadli Bendjedid is sworn in as president
OCT. 1988	October riots erupt due to dire economic situation and corruption
FEB. 23, 1989	New constitution is adopted that does away with the Algerian one-party system
SEPT. 16, 1989	Islamic Salvation Front is founded
JUNE 12, 1990	Islamic Salvation Front wins a majority in municipal elections
JAN. 11, 1992	The army cancels national elections, which were won by the Islamic Salvation Front; President Chadli Bendjedid resigns
FEB. 1992	Mohamed Boudiaf is appointed chairman of the High Council of State
JUNE 1992	Mohamed Boudiaf is assassinated by one of his bodyguards
1992–99	Algerian Civil War
1999	Abdelaziz Bouteflika is elected president
2011	The Arab Spring starts in Tunisia, and protests spread across the Arab world

1

Thursday, July 5, 2018

7:10 A.M.

"Karim. Karim! Karim!!"

Colonel Karim Soltani struggled to open his eyes and glanced at his watch. He scowled at Meriem, who had rudely awakened him from a pleasant slumber. She knew his sleep routine: 4 a.m. to 9 a.m. Any more or less and he'd be in a bad mood with a headache all day. He expressed his annoyance by pursing his lips, but she paid him no mind. Didn't he, like every other citizen of this country, have the right to enjoy a day off on Independence Day? He didn't dwell on it for too long since he realized a storm was brewing on the horizon. Meriem stood over him, tousling her long hair in extreme agitation.

"What is it?" he asked.

Sternly, she said, "Someone wants to speak with you."

"Here? Who is it?"

"He said it's the Big Boss."

At first, he thought she was joking, but Meriem's urgent tone convinced him to take her seriously. How did the Boss know he was there? And how dare he call him at this number? What could he possibly want this morning? Angrily, he dragged himself out of bed as if weighed down by dumbbells and headed to the living room to pick up the phone. No sooner had the word "hello" left his mouth than he was bombarded with a flood of choice insults and curses from the repertoire of General Brahim Belkacemi, the national champion of blasphemy, and also his direct superior in the Anti-Terrorism Unit. Soltani made it a habit of calling him "sir," unlike those fuckers who called him the Big Boss. Over time, he had become accustomed to dealing with him, trying to avoid confrontations as much as possible while not giving in too much.

"Good God, I've been looking everywhere for you. I'm in front of your place."

"What's the problem, sir?"

"I need to see you right away."

"What's happened? Has Judgment Day finally come?"

"Good God, Soltani. I'm no good with words and don't like talking more than I have to."

"I'll be there in fifteen minutes, sir."

He hung up the phone to avoid the next invective strike. He knew from experience that whenever the General repeated the phrase "good God," it was always followed by blasphemy, which irritated Soltani. He returned to the bedroom but didn't find Meriem there. He gathered up his scattered clothes and headed to the bathroom. After washing his face, he dressed and then glanced at himself in the mirror. Despite turning fifty-three months ago, he still looked like he was in his forties. He found her in the kitchen making coffee. He walked up to kiss her, but as she turned her head, she immediately yelled in his face, "Why did you give out my home phone number without my permission?!"

"Let me explain, Meryouma..."

"Get out of my house!"

He chose not to respond, having learned that continuing to talk with her in that state would only complicate things further. It was best to leave and let her cool down. Getting kicked out was no big deal; it wouldn't be the first time. How often had she thrown him out, only for them to make up later? What really infuriated him, though, was that he had done nothing wrong. He hadn't told anyone he was spending the night at Meriem's place. He wanted to defend himself but couldn't tell her the truth because Meriem was paranoid. She believed she was constantly under surveillance. Even though five years had passed since her divorce from her ex-husband, who had subjected her to relentless cruelty, she still hadn't escaped that nightmare.

Soltani snuck out through the small back gate to avoid the neighbors' attention. Divorced and living alone, Meriem had never returned to her family home, as most divorced women do. Thus, the eyes of those living in Gambetta never closed. The neighbors believed it was their right, no, their duty to watch over her to preserve the neighborhood's honor and integrity. He started the engine of his black 2012 Dacia Sandero that was parked at the end of the street and drove off. Oran's bewitching light, an effect of the sea and the sun, gave his heart a measure of tranquility.

The road to his downtown apartment, which overlooked the water, was almost empty compared to the usual unbearable traffic. The number of cars on the road in Oran was steadily increasing, while new road construction and repairs were painstakingly slow. He thought about how Algerians were so short-tempered. They didn't understand the meaning of patience, and the Boss and Meriem were no exceptions. He had just read about the rise in deaths in Algeria that came as a result of stress-induced heart attacks while driving. However, he didn't dwell on this; he turned his thoughts to Meriem. He often found himself grappling with conflicting emotions. On the one hand, he wanted to be with her because he loved her. On the other hand, he didn't want to sacrifice his freedom. Long-term relationships seemed risky, and marriage was something he wouldn't even consider, having failed at it before. In fact, he still incurred loss upon loss. His ex-wife, Nadia, never forgave him for the divorce and used every possible means to make his life difficult, using their son, Malik, as her most effective weapon against him. Just recently, Malik turned fifteen and, encouraged by his mother, turned down Soltani's gift of a new iPhone.

To get back at Soltani, she married a colleague who taught French with her at the high school two years after their divorce. When the matter of custody came up, Soltani carefully considered what would be best for his son. His demanding work schedule offered no scheduled days off, so he made the difficult decision to let his son live with his mother and her new husband. Instead of engaging in the typical battles of divorced couples, Soltani prioritized his son's well-being.

When he saw General Belkacemi standing alone in front of his sea-facing apartment building, thoughts of his ex-wife disappeared. Belkacemi had sent his driver on his way, meaning it was a sensitive matter. As soon as Soltani pulled over, the Boss jumped in without saying hello or anything.

"We don't have time. Go!"

"Where to, sir?"

"Saint-Hubert."

"What's there? Why did you call me at . . . ?"

"I'll tell you later. Right now, we have a disaster on our hands, Soltani."

"But I want to know now."

"Go, and I'll tell you everything."

Agitated, Soltani started the car and tore out. The General reprimanded him for always turning his cell phone off. He had been trying to reach him all morning, but without success. Finally, he had to call him on Meriem's home phone. Soltani could barely hide his anger. The Boss had to calm him down and explain that he had started keeping an eye on Meriem when he realized that Soltani's relationship with her was more serious than he had thought. Belkacemi assured him that he hadn't meant to spy on her or intrude on his personal life, but then he quickly changed his tone.

"You act like you're living in Sweden rather than Algeria. Here we have customs that are best followed, Soltani. And you mustn't underestimate her ex-husband, Shaaban Alili. He's dangerous and won't keep quiet."

He could have reminded him that Meriem wasn't under Alili's care. She was divorced and a free woman. He knew what Belkacemi's reply would be, so he saw no point in saying anything. Alili and creatures like him treated their ex-wives as their private property, off-limits to others. Meriem's ex-husband, a successful car salesman, fell into debt when he tried to edge out his competitors and expand his business. He had to leave the country and fled to Spain. Soltani tried to calm his nerves by taking out a pack of Nassims and lighting a cigarette, even though he knew the Boss had quit smoking two years ago and couldn't stand the smell.

"Do you want to know why we're going to Saint-Hubert or not?"

"I'm all ears."

"It has to do with Miloud Sabri."

"Hoopoe?"

"That's right."

"What'd he do, sir?"

"'Verily we belong to God, and to Him we shall return.'"

"He's dead?!"

The Boss plunged into the details without any preamble. Hoopoe was found an hour ago, killed, and in an awful state. There was intense pressure from the highest echelons to solve the crime as quickly as possible and keep it completely secret. There was a looming fear of a return to the civil war of the '90s—political assassinations, eliminating adversaries, and the reemergence of that old, troubling question: "Who killed whom?" The Colonel interrupted him to ask just one question: "Why did they put us in charge of this investigation?"

"Because we're the best there is, Soltani."

"That goes without saying. But why else, sir?"

"The higher-ups want to confirm whether or not the crime was an act of terrorism."

"I see."

General Belkacemi referred to the people in power as "higher-ups." Whether he meant the military or the Ministry of Defense or the secret police or the presidency, God only knew. The General didn't want to delve too deeply into it but hoped that the political assassination theory would not bear fruit; it wouldn't be an isolated episode but rather a long, boring rerun they had already seen. Soltani was convinced that the higher-ups did not relish a return to terrorism since the regional situation had changed entirely, and not for the better. In the '90s, the neighboring countries were stable. Now, Algeria is surrounded by conflagrations from Libya to Tunisia to Mali, and whoever plays with fire risks getting burned. In theory, if there were any differences among members of the higher-ups, they would necessarily be solved through the best available means; the benefits were substantial, and they would all get their share. There was no need to return to the old ways of eliminating adversaries, crying over them, and then placing the blame on terrorists.

When they got to Saint-Hubert, Soltani had no trouble parking the car in front of a magnificent colonial-era villa. There was no trace of the security forces, so he knew the crime was still being kept under wraps. He walked behind General Belkacemi, who rushed ahead, and they entered through the main gate. A large square garden filled with orange and lemon trees appeared before them. He cast a glance at the carefully and tastefully arranged flower beds, then bent over a red rose and caressed it, leaning in close to sniff its scent. He caught up with the General as he went up to the first floor, seeing an open door at the end of the hallway. He headed toward it and found himself in a spacious bedroom with a large balcony. Despite the open windows, the smell was awful. The first face he saw was that of the medical examiner, Abdou Hamlaoui, with traces of sleep still in his eyes. He had likely been told to hurry over and had no time to wash his face. A few steps into the room, the Colonel found himself face-to-face with the body. The victim was naked, hands and feet bound, lying in a mixture of blood, urine, and feces. He drew closer and saw that the tip of the man's nose had been placed on his chest, and that his throat had been slit from ear to ear. Then he noticed a man in his fifties by the window. He was fat, short, black-haired, and partially gray, stealing glances at the body, nervously touching his rounded beard, and crying silently. Soltani wondered who he was and what he was doing there. He didn't have to wonder for long. The General came over and whispered in his ear: Badreddine Bouzar, or Badrou for short. The dead man's son-in-law. He was the one who reported the crime.

After a little while, a team of three men dressed in white, resembling surgeons, approached and began examining the crime scene. They lifted fingerprints and took photographs of everything that could be photographed. As soon as one of them found a dagger covered in blood underneath the pillow, he handed it to the Boss, who then inspected it with Soltani after they had put on medical gloves. They concluded that the dagger was most likely the murder weapon. Badrou approached and stared at it, surprised and disturbed. Suddenly, he fainted, prompting the General to order someone to assist him immediately.

Soltani felt dizzy and rushed out of the room, almost throwing up. He realized he hadn't had his morning coffee yet, and his head was starting to pound. Belkacemi joined him and told him that the case was now his, that he was granting him full authority. Soltani stifled a laugh on hearing the word "authority" because he knew that everybody was responsible for protecting his own ass, no matter what "authority" was given.

The General insisted that no effort should be spared to achieve tangible results as quickly as possible. As he left, the Boss handed him a piece of paper.

"This's the address of Hoopoe's house."

"And what is *this* amazing place, sir?"

"This is the love nest. You need to go and speak with his wife, Zahra Misbah."

"May God guide His creatures!"

Soltani repeated this phrase whenever he found it difficult to find a reasonable explanation for something. He stuffed the piece of paper into his pocket and thought about the current housing crisis in Algeria. So many families in the big cities were jammed into one or two rooms like sardines, while others owned a villa for mistresses, another for their wife and children, and another for *their* children, and on and on.

Colonel Soltani called his aides, Captain Samir Ziane and First Lieutenant Malika Derraji, and instructed them to come meet him immediately without providing any explanation. He searched for a café nearby and was extremely lucky to find one that had opened that very day to coincide with Independence Day. The owner was giving away free drinks, and the coffee was good. He looked at the glass and saw the name "Lavazza" on it.

After that, Soltani went back to the villa and waited outside.

A half hour later, Captain Samir Ziane arrived. His good looks could not be missed; he was a handsome man in his late thirties, slim, tall, and light-skinned. Proud of his Kabyle accent. Ziane loved his job so much he would have worked without pay. He never followed orders precisely and loved taking the initiative, but as long as he did his job well and his luck held, he didn't attract any negative attention. And if he made a mistake, well, the courts and the gallows would be waiting for him. He followed his intuition and wasn't afraid of the consequences. In the eyes of bureaucrats, these faults made him a lost cause. However, Soltani considered these faults as positive qualities necessary for today's Anti-Terrorism officer. Terrorism had developed in such a way that keeping up with these things was a must. Ziane began working in

Colonel Soltani's unit five years ago. With his expertise in seven languages and knowledge of technology and hacking, he could access accounts and crack challenging codes. He spent long hours monitoring terrorist networks online. Ziane trusted the Colonel because he didn't leave him to face storms alone when the going got tough.

Colonel Soltani didn't reply to Captain Ziane's persistent questioning about why they had been called in so urgently on the morning of Independence Day. Soltani wanted to wait for Derraji to arrive so as not to have to repeat himself. There was nothing he hated more than repeating himself. How annoying that old saying was: "In repetition, there is benefit."

After a few minutes, First Lieutenant Malika Derraji showed up in her usual outfit of jeans, a T-shirt, and dark sunglasses. She looked like a university student even though she was thirty-one years old. Medium height. Brown-skinned with short hair. Ample bosom and a body that attracted unwelcome attention. When she walked the streets of Oran, there were always guys behind her, tongues hanging out, with something to say. Sexual repression in this city was as widespread as a cough in the winter. But Derraji was a romantic. She could not tolerate obscene comments and never ignored them, typically reprimanding the offender with a swift kick or a punch. If the lowlife understood the lesson and knew his limits, he'd be in luck, and all would be well. However, if he wished to seek revenge for his wounded masculinity because a young woman had just hit him in front of everyone, including the neighborhood kids, he would be forced to endure the pain mixed with humiliation. Derraji was a karate champion, and those who chose to fight back didn't discover this crucial piece of information until it was too late.

"Let's go examine the body and the crime scene," Soltani said to his two aides.

They went up to the victim's room, where the summer heat had worsened the unbearable smell. Soltani tried to keep the examination short, so he focused on the slit throat and the severed tip of the nose. He pointed to the dagger that had been found underneath the victim's pillow. He only spoke the victim's name when he was done and they could no longer bear the suspense. Miloud Sabri was not just anyone. Everyone knew him by his nickname, Hoopoe, which always preceded him wherever he went. Derraji reviewed the summary information on him. She had an excellent memory and could recall even the smallest details. She referred to an investigative article she had read years ago in a newspaper containing information about Hoopoe's role in the Algerian Revolution. He had been part of a guerrilla group, which included Zahra Misbah, aka Dolores, who became his wife after independence, and the well-known human rights activist and lawyer Driss Talbi, aka Falcon. As for the fourth group member, the article only mentioned his nickname, Stork. He was shrouded in mystery. It is said that he was an embedded agent. He may have fled with the French or perished at the hands of revolutionaries from the Liberation Front just before independence.

Colonel Soltani made it a habit of reviewing initial theories with his aides to establish the right course and set a plan of action. A successful investigation depends on grasping the essential threads of the case. Here, he said, there were two. He stopped talking and pushed the door of interpretation wide open.

"The timing, sir," said Ziane.

"The slaughter and cutting off the tip of the nose, sir," Derraji added.

Carrying out the operation on Independence Day was meant to sabotage the celebratory mood. The method of killing—slitting the throat and cutting off the tip of the nose—was a practice started by the Liberation Front during the Revolution to punish traitors and those who disobeyed orders. Soltani smiled approvingly at the two answers and concluded that both threads led directly to the War of Independence. He emphasized the importance of the nose to Algerians, as it symbolizes integrity. Anyone who can't sniff out the rot in their home and surroundings has no nose and lacks honor. Was the slaughter of Miloud Sabri a settling of old accounts? What was intended by leaving the dagger at the crime scene? Why was the tip of the nose placed on the victim's chest? Soltani tossed these questions out as a pregame warm-up.

Colonel Soltani instructed his aides to gather as much information as possible on Miloud Sabri. Initially, he encouraged them to compete with one another and then cooperate and divide the work between them. He could see they were enthusiastic and focused, like two eagles preparing for the hunt.

2

Autumn 1958

Miloud Sabri, aka Hoopoe, arrived at the emergency meeting in the storeroom of the Ifri Bakery in the old neighborhood of Medina Jedida. He found his three friends, Zahra Misbah, aka Dolores; Driss Talbi, aka Falcon; and Abbas Badi, aka Stork, waiting for him. He could not hide his agitation, and his comrades understood that something serious had happened. As soon as the door closed behind him, Hoopoe informed them that the police had arrested their direct superior, Yazid Mansouri, the night before.

"No!" screamed Dolores, covering her mouth with her hand.

"How did they get to him?" Stork asked.

"Someone ratted on him, brother," Hoopoe replied.

"Who?" wondered Falcon.

"One of us... so they say." Hoopoe uttered these three words as he looked around at each of them to gauge their reactions.

The news hit them hard. Betrayal of a secret operation was certainly possible, and exchanging intelligence was a common practice among infiltrators. But it was difficult to accept that the traitor was one of them. Hoopoe said that Omar Mansouri, Yazid's direct superior and cousin, was the one accusing them because only *they* knew the location of his last hiding place.

They all talked at once, except for Dolores, who took refuge in silence. It was her habit to swallow her words when things got intense. She was afraid her tears would betray her and make her appear weak. As for Hoopoe, he was only focused on one thing, that their lives were now in danger. Yazid knew who they were, and he might confess under torture. Who knows? The search may already have begun. They had to get out of sight and take refuge in new hideouts immediately. They faced another problem as well. If the one who had ratted on Yazid was one of them, it was obvious that they had to suspend their trust in one another until things became clearer.

They decided to leave the hideout for good and stay away from one another until further notice. Hiding and closely monitoring the situation were basic priorities in dealing with emergency situations such as this. Yazid *might* remain steadfast under torture, and their identities would remain unknown to the colonial authorities. Only then would they be able to return to guerrilla operations, after being reassured of his silence, of course. This last scenario was possible if remote; French investigators were well-trained and possessed the latest interrogation tools and techniques. Who could hold out forever?

There was no question they had to split up and go their separate ways. They pulled themselves together to keep from crying, as they might never see one another again. This feeling so overwhelmed them that they focused on saving themselves before it was too late. Remaining clear-headed in these types of situations is difficult and complicated, but they tried to project determination and enthusiasm, softly taking up their mantra:

"Long live Algeria! Long live Algeria! Long live Algeria!"

Then, in hushed voices, they started to sing.

My brothers, don't forget the martyrs
who sacrificed themselves for the life of the country.
With tears and blood, they protected your land.
They left family, friends, and children.
Their voices, from the grave, call out to you.
Listen, people, to this voice:
Unity is our watchword.
Sacrifice is our means.
Freedom is our goal.
Long live Algeria!

Falcon left first while Hoopoe watched from the small window overlooking the street. Dolores walked toward the door after the tears streaming down her face had dried and she had hugged Stork, who walked out behind her. Hoopoe waited five minutes before leaving the storeroom, which had been their safe haven for a full year. He headed to the Canastel district to hide out on the farm of a Liberation Front member.

Miloud Sabri loved Canastel. It looked out over the sea and lay next to a large, beautiful forest. He first visited it when he was ten, accompanying his father, who worked as a gardener at a villa owned by a famous wine producer named Bernard Clavel. On that particular day, the owners of the house were on vacation in Spain, so the servant—they used to call her Fatma, as most French settlers called their servants—showed him around the house. And he saw the wonder of it all: a luxurious reception hall, spacious bedrooms overlooking the sea, bathtubs, and balconies covered with flowers. He imagined himself in the paradise he heard so much about. On their way home, Miloud asked his father,

"Why are we so poor and the French so rich?"

"Such is the wisdom of the Lord, my son."

"Meaning our Lord is unjust?"

"God forbid! Another word and you'll get the rod!"

Miloud remained silent the rest of the way home so his father would not make good on his threat. All the amazing things he had seen in the Clavel villa played back repeatedly in his head. He never forgot them. Little did he know that fate would bring him back to that very house six years later to replace his father, who fell from the top of an orange tree and, as a result, lost his ability to walk. Miloud was forced to quit high school and take his father's place. He was the oldest son, and there was no one else to provide for the family. Clavel was not a merciful man. He forced Miloud's father to bear the consequences of the tragic accident and only begrudgingly gave in to the family's pleas not to cut off their livelihood by agreeing to try Miloud out for two weeks.

"If you can't do it, I'll look for another gardener, and he sure won't be an Arab! I'm sick and tired of you all. Understood, Mohamed?"

"My name is Miloud, Monsieur Clavel."

"As far as I'm concerned, you all are either Mohamed or Fatma. Understood?"

"Yes, Monsieur Clavel."

He worked hard to learn the basics of the job and passed the test with no problem. Then, little by little, he grew accustomed to the insults and racist slurs that Monsieur Clavel and his precious wife would hurl.

In the summer of 1956, terribly affected by the guillotining of his neighbor, Ahmed Zabana, Miloud joined the National Liberation Front as a messenger and took on the nom de guerre of Hoopoe. Yazid Mansouri showed him the first issue of the clandestine newspaper *El Moudjahid*, which published Zabana's farewell letter to his family. Hoopoe wept as he read it over and over again until he had memorized it.

> My dear relatives, my precious mother:
> As I write this, I do not know whether this letter will be my last. Only God knows. Something terrible has happened to me, but do not despair of God's mercy.

> Death for the sake of God is an endless life. And death for the sake of the nation is a duty. You have performed your duty by sacrificing the dearest of your creations, so do not weep for me. Take pride in me. Accept the greetings of a son and a brother who always loved you and who was always loved by you. They might be my last greetings to you.

At first, Hoopoe took part in guerrilla operations such as planting bombs in places frequented by Europeans. His mission was to provide logistical support only. He was extremely focused and noticed every detail, always in full control of his nerves. This is what encouraged Yazid to put his trust in him, and in the spring of 1957, he was charged with carrying out his first significant mission near the Central Post Office. Yazid told him that the target was a police officer who specialized in torturing guerrilla fighters and their families; he was in the habit of spending his Wednesday evenings in an eyeglass shop owned by a friend of his, located on Place de la Bastille. Hoopoe followed orders to the letter and stuck to the established protocol: arrive fifteen minutes early, wait until the appointed time, then wait another fifteen minutes. If the person you are supposed to meet does not show, leave and don't come back, temporarily cutting off communications until further notice.

He stood at the main door of the Central Post Office on the appointed day. An attractive young woman in a white summer dress and blue stockings approached him.

"What a surprise!" she exclaimed.

Hoopoe feigned surprise and said in a loud voice, "Dolores!"

They exchanged kisses and started talking like old friends who had not seen each other for some time. After a few minutes, she asked him to join her. They walked calmly toward the target, joking and laughing. When they arrived at the shop door, Hoopoe put his hand into her small purse, which he found open. Coolly, he removed the grenade and walked up to the shop's entrance. He pulled out the pin and tossed it inside. They hurried away, and when they heard the grenade explode, they took off running, each in a different direction. The next day, Hoopoe learned that the officer was killed, while his friend was in critical condition. Hoopoe had thought he wouldn't be able to sleep after killing someone for the first time, but he slept calmly that night, undisturbed by nightmares or remorse.

At first, Hoopoe thought Dolores was a European sympathetic to the Algerian Communist Party. However, two weeks after the operation, he learned that Dolores was the alias of an Algerian woman named Zahra Misbah, a student at the Stephane Gsell Girls' High School. Anyone seeing her without knowing her would have thought she was European. She carefully imitated European girls' way of speaking and manner of dress. She didn't need to show identification papers for people to be convinced she was European, especially given her mastery of Spanish. Her beauty was her essential asset; her innocent face and open smile were her tools of seduction. Hoopoe fell in love with Dolores early on, but he kept his feelings to himself, accustomed as he was to being patient and not playing his cards all at once. He was waiting for the right moment.

The police stormed the family homes of Dolores, Hoopoe, Falcon, and Stork in search of them. It was clear that Yazid had stuck to a Liberation Front rule: Remain steadfast for two days before confessing. With that, the hunt officially began, and remaining in Oran became dangerous. Hoopoe was able to cross the Algerian–Moroccan border with the help of a Moroccan merchant. He stayed in Oujda for three days and made contact with a cell associated with the Liberation Front who sent him to Casablanca. There he joined the ranks of Abdelhafid Boussouf, and thus began his adventures with the first seeds of the Algerian intelligence services.

Dolores was proud to come from Sidi Houari, where different communities, cultures, and religions lived together peacefully, unlike other neighborhoods in the city. Oran's residents were distributed in the following way: Muslims in Medina Jedida and Hamri, and Jews in the street behind the opera building. The wealthy Europeans lived in luxury apartments in the middle of the city or villas in Saint-Hubert, Les Palmiers, and Canastel. As for the poor Europeans, most of them Spanish and Italian, they lived in mixed neighborhoods such as Gambetta, Eckmühl, and Sidi Houari.

From the time she was a little girl, she had attached herself to the family of her neighbors, Pablo Garcia

Mendez and his wife, Carmen. They were Spanish Republican Communists who had taken refuge in Oran in 1936, having fled Franco's hell. She became friends with their three children, Rosita, Juanito, and Carlos, and learned Spanish from them. Zahra always felt that she was a part of the family. The head of the household, Pablo Garcia, who worked as a stevedore at the port, called her "Dolores" after the communist hero Isadora Dolores Ibárruri Gómez, famously known as "la Pasionaria." He considered her a second daughter and would often joke with her, "The blood of Spaniards runs through your veins, Dolores."

"Maybe Andalusian blood, Uncle Pablo."

"Yes, so true."

But she always bristled at the praise directed at her, which carried a whiff of discrimination and racism. "You're European like us." "You're completely different." "You're a model to follow." "You're the symbol of France's success in this country."

A specific event from childhood stuck in her memory and left a permanent mark. On the final exam for her elementary school certificate, she received the highest grade. Her close friend, Françoise, came in a close second, which caused her to burst into tears. Zahra tried to comfort her, and after a long sigh, Françoise explained what was so upsetting.

"How can I tell my mother that a Muslim did better than me?"

She was so insulted, she ended the friendship right there.

Zahra, using "Dolores" as her nom de guerre, joined the Algerian guerrilla fighters in 1957. Her sister Farida, who was a year older, was already a member. Then, her brother Youssef, two years younger, followed suit. Despite his youth, he played an active role in communications between the freedom fighters. Yazid, their neighbor in Sidi Houari, was the one who had drafted the three siblings.

Dolores and Hoopoe carried out several successful operations together. They were very comfortable with one another, as if they were engaged to be married or were European lovers. They possessed an unusual calmness, which led Yazid to assign them the most complex and risky operations. One time, as Hoopoe was about to kill a traitor who was cooperating with the French, the dagger fell from his hand. Dolores didn't hesitate for a single moment. She grabbed the dagger and, instead of handing it back to Hoopoe, walked up to the traitor and plunged it into his stomach three times, killing him.

Dolores was able to flee Oran with the help of Pablo Garcia. As he drove the car to Relizane, where members of the Liberation Front were waiting to take her to the mountains, he said to her in Spanish, "I don't want to know what you did, Dolores."

"I just did what needed to be done, Uncle Pablo."

"If that's how it is, then fine," he responded, smiling.

Driss Talbi, aka Falcon, chose to remain in Oran and continue the armed struggle there, but he was arrested and tortured. He was put on trial and sentenced to death, incarcerated in the Casbah prison in Oran. Of course, the guillotine was not the only way one could die. So many freedom fighters died under torture, but Falcon was spared this fate thanks to Jean Moulin, a hero of the French resistance against the Nazis. One time, Falcon was being questioned by a French inspector who was not quite as brutal as his colleagues. There was something in his eyes and the way he acted that made him seem different. Between torture sessions, Falcon stood before his interrogators.

"Your nickname is Falcon, right?"

"Yes, Monsieur Inspector."

"How'd you get it?"

"I wasn't afraid of fighting the older kids when I was younger."

"One of the falcon's traits is courage, but you're a coward because you're a terrorist. You strike and then run away."

"No, Monsieur Inspector, I'm a resistance fighter like Jean Moulin."

"Really?!"

The Inspector told him that he, too, had been a resistance fighter during the Second World War and that he was arrested and tortured in the Gestapo's prison cells. After that, he started to treat Falcon better.

At first, the Inspector convinced himself that torture was necessary to stop the explosions in public places and the killing of innocent civilians. But the ugliness of the daily torture sessions and memories of the Gestapo that they brought back to the surface led to a nervous breakdown. During their final meeting, he said, "Today, my position in the game has changed."

"The position of good is obvious, Monsieur Inspector, as is the position of evil."

"Really? I used to think like you."

"Good must triumph in the end."

"Do you really think it's possible to defeat evil?"

"I have no doubt that it is, Monsieur Inspector."

"But evil is fertile."

"No, quite the opposite is true, Monsieur Inspector."

"Don't you see that the victims learn the art of torture from their torturers?" said the Inspector fighting back tears.

Falcon took the Inspector's words to heart and hoped they would not be tested one day.

The fates of Miloud, Driss, and Abbas were linked from the time they were born, a year before the start of the Second World War. They were guided into the world by the hand of Dr. Jean-Marie Larribère, who had brought the natural childbirth method to Algeria. They grew up together in Place de Sidi Bilal in the heart of Medina Jedida, or "Negroville," as the Europeans called it. General Lamoricière had built it in 1845 to house those who migrated to Oran from the surrounding villages. However, the real purpose was to contain and keep watch over them so they could not provide any assistance to the revolutionaries as they had done before with the anti-colonial leader Emir Abdelkader.

They memorized chapters from the Qur'an in the same Qur'anic school, and they attended the same public schools. They shared the bitter and the sweet from a young age, and their friendship was the envy of all. The first picture taken of them dates back to the day of their circumcision when they were four years old. They were laughing, unaware that the scissors of the barber, Hadj Boualem, would bring tears to their eyes soon after the picture was taken. There's another picture of them at fourteen, arms around one another in Tahtaha, the largest square in Medina Jedida. Abbas, the tallest, is in the middle, with Miloud to his right and the shortest one, Driss, on the left. Fort Santa Cruz can be seen behind them, and to their right and left, there are about forty cafés. People would choose a café according to what music they liked to listen to: Cheikh Hamada, Cheikh El Khaldi, Reinette L'Oranaise, Cheikha Tetma, Umm Kulthum, Mohamed Abdel Wahab. Their ears grew accustomed to the clamor of people's voices in their neighborhood. With its famous market, Sidi Okba, and its cheap hotels, bathhouses, and cafés, Medina Jedida attracted visitors from far and wide to Oran.

When they were teenagers, the three friends all experienced their first awkward sexual encounters during an unforgettable evening between the thighs of a woman named Cherifa. She was a prostitute from Sidi Bel Abbès, who, when she got older, settled down in Sidi Houari, determined to retire and repent. However, she would return to her old profession whenever life forced her to. Thanks to her, the three young men discovered the secrets of the female body and the ABCs of kissing, hugging, and sex.

During their first year at Ardaillon High School, they became close with their history teacher, Pierre Rondeau. He was an admirer of Albert Camus, who had studied under him during the writer's stay in Oran in 1941 and 1942. He was especially fond of his famous novel, *The Stranger.* He once described the crime of Meursault, the novel's main character, as that of one brother killing another.

"But Meursault didn't kill a Frenchman. He killed a nameless Arab," remarked Driss.

"The nameless Arab was a native of this country, just like Meursault. They were brothers like Cain and Abel," replied the teacher.

Born in Algeria, Professeur Rondeau was descended from a family that had emigrated from Alsace-Lorraine in the north of France and settled in the Algerian west after France's defeat against Germany in 1871. When the spark of the War of Independence was lit in November 1954, he remained optimistic that things would return to normal and security would be reestablished, but on the condition that the European minority accept the profound reforms that would benefit the Muslim majority. However, Muslim Algerians did not enjoy the benefits of citizenship. They were subject to the Native Code of 1881, which granted the French military authorities broad powers to punish the "natives" for the most trivial of reasons without recourse to the judicial system.

Despite these difficulties and obstacles, Professeur Rondeau liked to quote Camus: "We are sentenced to live together." But the struggle intensified. On one side, the French government thought it could resolve the situation militarily, sending close to half a million soldiers to Algeria. On the other side, the Liberation Front was sure Algeria would be freed from the shackles of colonialism, especially after two neighboring countries, Morocco and Tunisia, achieved independence in 1956.

Miloud, Driss, and Abbas would visit Professeur Rondeau in his apartment in Plateau Saint-Michel on weekends. There, they met his wife, who was fundamentally different from her husband, and they would watch them argue about the situation in Algeria. Madame Madelaine Rondeau was also born in Oran and worked as a pediatrician. She was utterly convinced that the root of all the problems there was the failure of integration. She was convinced that France had not gotten its message of "civilization" across in Algeria because it had not closed the mosques, liberated women from the hijab, or banned the teaching of the Qur'an. She would constantly repeat her favorite adage: "Islam is like a rotten molar. No use treating it."

Professeur Rondeau would double down whenever his wife started expounding her theories of Islam. He would ask her with disdain, "What's the last Western movie you watched, my dear?"

Professeur Rondeau would refer to Westerns when he argued with his wife because she loved them so much. He reminded her of something she had said a few months prior during a dinner with family and friends.

"If France had followed America's model of occupation, we wouldn't find ourselves forced into war today. Civilizing people is a serious and costly enterprise."

"Forget about the American Indians, my dear. We need serious reforms today," replied a somewhat agitated Professeur Rondeau.

He then reminded the guests seated around the dinner table that France had squandered numerous chances to improve the situation of the native population, starting with the Cremieux Decree of 1870, which granted citizenship to Jews but not Muslims. Then there was the Blum-Violette Proposal of 1936, which sought to ease the process of gaining citizenship for some, but not all Muslims. The French inhabitants of Algeria, led by colonists and property owners, stood together against that proposal and ensured its failure.

The three friends ran into Madame Rondeau the day after General de Gaulle's first visit to Oran in June 1958. She could not have been happier and mentioned that she was among the thousands of people who had welcomed him. She had heard the General's pronouncement with her own two ears: "France is here, charged with its mission, and will be here forever!"

Madame Rondeau added with unrivaled enthusiasm that the final victory was near and that French Algeria was secure. Professeur Rondeau, who was completely opposed to this point of view, did not hide his pessimism and sadness as he said, "Peace is growing ever more distant. De Gaulle is a military man, and his profession is war."

Like Miloud, Abbas Badi dropped out of high school to help his father in a jewelry-making shop in Medina Jedida, and he became quite good at it. Driss stayed in high school and graduated. Abbas and Driss took up arms in the fall of 1957 and came to be known as Stork and Falcon from then on. They had to follow the directives of the Liberation Front that mandated that before joining any armed unit, they had to kill a European directly involved in the colonial administration. The purpose of this test was to guard against any attempts at infiltrating the ranks of the Liberation Front. Stork passed the test by stabbing a soldier in the neck near Place de la Victoire, while Falcon did so by putting a hand grenade in a seaside restaurant.

Stork met Zahra, aka Dolores, at a preparation meeting for a joint guerrilla operation. He was immediately drawn to her. One time, he said jokingly, "I don't like the name Zahra."

"Why not?"

"It's not right. It means 'flower,' but one flower isn't enough."

"So, what do you suggest?"

"Zuhour! Flowers! From now on I'll call you Zuhour."

"As you like," she responded with a smile.

Stork always looked forward to seeing her. He stammered whenever he talked with her. He noticed that she behaved differently with him; her eyes revealed things she was too shy to express, and he was soon convinced that they shared the same feelings.

"I want to learn Spanish and flamenco dancing," Stork said one day, feigning seriousness.

"What's preventing you?"

"Until now, I haven't found anyone to teach me."

"There are so many teachers."

"You need to know that I insist on two necessary qualifications," added Stork.

"And they are . . . ?"

"The teacher has to be a woman."

"And the other condition?"

"She has to be absolutely beautiful."

"You won't easily find a teacher, then," she commented.

"But thank God, I have found her."

"Where?"

"Standing right here in front of me!"

She blushed, then smiled. They started meeting secretly in different places for Spanish and flamenco lessons, and to exchange furtive kisses. After six months, Stork decided to ask Hoopoe and Falcon for advice.

"Zahra and I have decided to get married."

"Congratulations!" said Falcon.

"Have you spoken with Si Yazid?" asked Hoopoe.

"No, not yet, but you can at least congratulate me, Hoopoe."

"A thousand congratulations, brother," Hoopoe rushed to say, hiding his embarrassment behind a smile.

Stork broached the subject with their superior, Yazid, who asked that they delay things so they could attend to more pressing matters. The time was not right for thinking about marriage. Yazid cautioned Stork to stay focused, emphasizing that mistakes were costly and affected not only the person making them, but also his brothers-in-arms. Stork was not convinced, and for good reason. Yazid had recently married. Things escalated, and Stork retorted with a mixture of sarcasm and anger, "Okay for you, but not for us."

In the end, Stork reluctantly gave in to reality and decided he would try again in the not-so-distant future.

On the same day that news reached him that Yazid had died under torture, Stork was able to leave Oran and join some other freedom fighters in Mascara. The whole time he was on the run, he could not shake the thought that Yazid might have confessed and given away the location of their hiding place and that they would all be arrested.

When the four comrades parted ways after that last meeting, they were unable to rid themselves of the specter of betrayal and some troubling questions: Was Yazid a victim of betrayal? Was the traitor one of them? Would they ever discover the truth?

3

Thursday, July 5, 2018

9:40 A.M.

After the Italian coffee, Colonel Karim Soltani's mind regained its focus. As he drove through the emptier-than-usual streets, he gazed at the palm trees planted on the sides of the roads in recent years to beautify the city; some of them had died while others still lived. He often likened himself to a palm tree that acclimates easily to its environment. He had been uprooted from Algiers, where he was born, and replanted in the magnificent city of Oran. When he was first sent there in 1993 to carry out his military service, he was astonished by the Oranians' joie de vivre, and he was now so attached to the place that he could not live anywhere else.

He shook himself out of his reverie about Oran and focused on the preliminary information and questions at hand surrounding the crime. Was the fact that Miloud, aka Hoopoe, was slaughtered on Independence Day purely a coincidence? And why was the dagger found underneath the pillow? The Colonel did not like the word "coincidence." Whenever people found themselves unable to understand something, they were quick to hide behind coincidences and fate, and prophetic hadiths such as, "God has decreed, and what He has willed, has come to pass." His expertise, especially when investigating terrorist crimes, had taught him that looking into chance occurrences was often the shortest path to finding the perpetrators. But was this crime connected to terrorism in any way? Perhaps. If the killer was a terrorist, the primary purpose was not to do away with just one enemy. The real goal was to spread fear and terror among the greatest possible number of people. If this theory was correct, then Hoopoe's killing would not be the last. Others would follow. Just as he had many times before, he asked himself what exactly terrorism was. He always arrived at different definitions, but in the end, he agreed with the prevailing wisdom that terrorism was a form of killing in installments. Every day, terrorists kill something of value in people's souls. Sometimes it's their hopes, sometimes their courage, sometimes their dreams, and so on. He had become an expert on how terrorists think; in the '90s he served on the front lines fighting terrorism in western Algeria. After that, his duties expanded to include the rest of the country and abroad as well.

After considering the timing of the crime, he moved on to its location: the Mistress's Villa. Did Hoopoe own it? Mind you, he was not asking just to find out what Hoopoe owned, thus applying the accusatory principle of "Where did you get this?" He knew that no one kept track of such things in this country. "You scratch my back, and I'll scratch yours," as the bastards say. Bribery, a cup of coffee, or a "tip"—as the corrupt Islamists refer to it—can be found in every corner of this country. Neither injunctions nor religious values have worked to eradicate this scourge, not even to limit its spread. Everyone knows bribery is haram, forbidden, but there's a difference between belief and practice, words and actions.

Until now, he had been able to fight off bribery and corruption, which he was proud of. He had kept his distance from the trap of using connections as much as possible because he knew that was the first step down a slippery slope. Every service has its price. This stance caused a great many problems between him and his family, first and foremost. Four years ago, his oldest brother was sent to prison for embezzling from the bank where he worked. The evidence against him was beyond the slightest doubt. Nevertheless, his mother and brothers pressured Soltani to intervene and help get him out, but he refused, which made his mother explode in anger.

"You neither benefited yourself nor helped any one of us!"

His relationship with his family deteriorated to the point where he was completely estranged, ostracized, no longer invited to family celebrations. Last year, after completing his sentence, his brother found the embezzled money waiting for him. He bought a villa and a luxury car for which no one held him accountable. Cases like these were all too common. So many bank employees took the risk of embezzling, even factoring in the possibility of arrest, knowing that the good life awaited them as soon as they got out of prison. The Colonel's hatred for corruption did not stem from religious obligation or high morals. Rather, it stemmed from his pride in himself, for how satisfying it felt when he could say to anyone who tried to bribe him, "Karim Soltani is not for sale!"

He arrived at Hoopoe's address in Canastel, a neighborhood that was in a state of constant change. The beautiful old villas with their magnificent gardens were ceding space to a hodgepodge of ugly buildings. He parked his car at the entrance to a gorgeous villa overlooking the sea, and as soon as he got out, he saw an angry man with missing front teeth screaming from a small window in a security booth.

"Take this clunker and get out of here!"

"Should I knock out what's left of your teeth?" the Colonel threatened.

"This place is off-limits."

"I don't like repeating myself, Mr. Clunker," Soltani growled.

He calmly got out of the car and smoothed his shirt. The guard seemed to have noticed the Caracal F semiautomatic pistol he had concealed on his left side and rushed to apologize, but Soltani ignored him. He figured the fucker had treated him with such disdain because of his old car. Had he been in a luxury car, the guard would have opened the door with a smile, strewn red roses out in front of him, and welcomed him with open arms. In this country though, appearances, especially cars, had become everything. Tell me what car you drive, and I'll tell you who you are.

"Tell Madame Misbah that Colonel Soltani wants to speak with her." He uttered these words in a blasé manner without even looking at the guard.

"Right away, sir."

The guard accompanied him to the living room, where a handsome, slim man in his early seventies was waiting. The man wore a Rolex on his right wrist and a gold bracelet on his left. He walked toward Soltani amiably and told him he had just received a call from the Boss letting him know he was coming.

"I am Youssef Misbah. Miloud's brother-in-law."

"Pleased to meet you, Mr. Misbah."

The man welcoming him in was not unknown to Soltani. He had heard of him but had not met him before. He was a hero of the Revolution, a distinguished freedom fighter in Oran who made trouble for the colonial authorities despite his young age, and who always managed to slip through their fingers. He retired from the intelligence service in the late '90s and got involved in business and commerce, as many retired officers do. Colonel Soltani learned from him that his sister was still in shock, so he promised to keep it short. Misbah asked him to wait in the sitting room and went upstairs.

Youssef returned five minutes later with his sister, a woman in her seventies wearing a hijab, who defied the years with her grace and beauty. She extended her hand, shook his, and invited him into her office. She asked her brother to leave them alone. The brother withdrew somewhat reluctantly; he seemed surprised by the request. The Colonel did not want to waste any time on formalities, so as soon as they sat down on two comfortable sofas, he asked her about the last time she had seen the deceased. She replied that she had eaten lunch with him the previous day, and then he called her on the phone that evening. He stared into the widow's eyes before casting his line like a skilled fisherman.

"Tell me, madame. The villa where your husband died. Is it yours?"

"God only knows."

"What do you mean 'God only knows,' madame?!"

She looked at him as if surprised by the question.

"Like millions of other Algerian women, I don't know all of my husband's secrets."

He pretended to be convinced by her explanation but did not stop asking questions.

"Did the deceased have any enemies?"

"We all have enemies. Even the Almighty God has them. That's life."

"Right you are, Madame Dolores."

"Dolores! You have good information, Colonel."

"It's my job, madame."

Soltani thought that perhaps he had scored a point in his favor. Would the widow change her manner of speaking and treat him with the respect he deserved, or would she continue with this game of cat and mouse? Luckily, the widow appeared to think well of him. She asked him whether he wanted coffee or tea. This was a good sign. He immediately concluded that she wanted to prolong the conversation and promptly chose coffee. Perhaps she would reveal something, and he was a good listener. The

Colonel worked according to one of the few sayings he liked: "Go meet your Lord naked, and he will clothe you." There was no use in playing games. Madame Zahra, aka Dolores, was an unusual woman. It must not have been easy for a woman younger than twenty to participate in operations that involved carrying weapons and bombs and killing people. She must have been quite courageous and skilled. He informed the widow of his initial findings in the investigation. When he described the murdered man's body to her in detail, he noticed that she remained composed. Perhaps she did not want to show the effect this had on her.

"The crime is a settling of old accounts, madame."

"I don't understand."

"Revenge."

"What do you mean?"

"Revenge that has something to do with the Revolution, Madame Dolores."

"Does revenge make sense after more than half a century has passed? I'm not convinced."

She stopped talking when she heard knocks on the door. A woman in her sixties came in and placed a tray with two cups of coffee and two glasses of water on the table. She waited for the servant to leave, then began to talk about her guerrilla activities and how she joined the Revolution. It had been extremely difficult for her. On the one hand, she had to face her fear of the French police, and on the other hand, the weight of social traditions. Her father was not at all pleased when he found out his daughter was bearing arms. In fact, he scolded her, "War is for men."

Dolores took a sip of coffee, then looked straight at Soltani and said, "I don't like to don lawyers' robes."

"In whose defense, madame?"

"Guerrilla action, Mr. Soltani. There are some Algerians who have come to consider it a form of terrorism. Guerrilla activities are one way of *fighting* terrorism. Was not colonialism in and of itself a terrorist aggression? Self-defense is a legally protected right. The torture, executions, assassinations, and use of napalm to kill civilians that occurred under colonialism amount to much more than what's attributed to guerrillas. That's why we have to distinguish between the perpetrator and the victim, between the aggressor and the one acting in self-defense, between the terrorist and the guerrilla freedom fighter. Am I wrong?"

She did not wait for a response, as if the question were rhetorical. "Do you want my frank opinion?" she asked.

"I do."

"There's terrorism that's acceptable, and there's terrorism that's reprehensible."

"How so, madame?"

"If you had lived through that time, you wouldn't ask that question. What I *can* say is that, when carrying out those guerrilla operations, I would picture the Algerian victims. Children, for example. This would help me free myself from feelings of pity or pangs of guilt. As for killing traitors, there is no need for any pity whatsoever. Spilling the blood of traitors is halal, permissible!"

She repeated the last sentence in a grave voice, her eyes betraying her mercilessness and bitter hatred.

Soltani listened to what the widow was saying and did not find anything new in it. No regret for killing Europeans, not even unarmed civilians. Like others, she played the self-defense or acceptable terrorism card, concluding that violence begets violence and that terrorism begets terrorism. He felt that he was straying from the matter at hand. He did not come in search of the historical truth and the final word in what were extremely thorny moral questions such as whether terrorism, with all of its justifications, was acceptable or not. This question was both old and new at the same time. Despite his full engagement with this problem, he had not yet come to a clear and comprehensive answer. He asked the widow for information about her former guerrilla group.

"What do you want to know, my son? You're around the same age as my daughters Mona and Souad."

"May God protect them."

"And have mercy on those who have died."

Dolores stopped talking, and the tears welled up. She composed herself, reaching for a handkerchief to nervously dry her eyes. Apologizing, she explained that her youngest daughter, Souad, had been assassinated by terrorists in 1998. She turned abruptly, picked up a framed picture from a shelf behind her, and handed it to him. It was a picture of a beautiful, smiling young woman in her early twenties with the Eiffel Tower in the background.

"The ugliest, most miserable pain you can feel is to bury your child with your own hands. Children should be burying their parents, not vice versa."

"So true, madame."

The widow regained her composure and returned to talking about her former comrades.

"What do you want to know about the group?"

"You were four. You, your deceased husband, and the lawyer Driss Talbi, aka Falcon. Who was the fourth, known only as 'Stork'?"

"Abbas Badi... may God have mercy on him."

"He died?"

"I don't know..."

"You just said 'may God have mercy on him,' madame."

Dolores looked uneasy for the first time as she spoke about Stork. The Colonel felt that her appetite for talking was just about gone. He understood that it was time to go, so he got up and excused himself. He thanked her for agreeing to meet and answer his questions despite the sad circumstances. He gave her his number, asking her to give him a call if she remembered anything important or otherwise wanted to get in touch. He shook her hand, expressed his condolences again, and walked out of the room. As he was heading toward the gate, he came face to face with Nabil Talbi. Everything about him was long: his stature, his hair, his nose, and his tongue (oh, how he liked to talk!). He was the managing director of the Horriya Media Group, which owned a newspaper and television station by the same name. Soltani was surprised this journalist was here. Who told him about Hoopoe's murder? Had word of the case gotten out? Would Horriya TV be the first to broadcast the news? Even before the state news agency?

Nabil Talbi put his hand out to greet the Colonel, but the Colonel ignored it. Nabil understood that Soltani had not forgotten their argument two years earlier when his newspaper published an article about an anti-terrorism operation and developments related to it before the investigation was complete. At that time, Soltani was furious and wanted to know who had leaked the information, but it was no use. He was unable to break Nabil through threats and pressure. Nabil refused to reveal his source, and the Colonel realized that the journalist had the backing of influential people in powerful positions. Back then a colleague advised him to let it go: "'Piss on him,' as the Tunisians say."

That was not so easy for Colonel Soltani, who didn't forget so easily.

The Colonel passed through the villa's gate and found the guard cleaning his car's mirrors. He ordered him to move away, or else he would make good on his previous threat to knock his teeth out. The poor fellow took a few steps back and nearly fell down, he was so scared. Soltani got into his car and took off toward his office downtown. He turned on the radio and became engrossed in a discussion about the Europeans who fought for Algeria's independence and whether it was right to call those who died "martyrs." Or were the words "martyr" and "freedom fighter" the sole monopoly of Muslim Algerians? One of the speakers mentioned the case of the socialist militant Fernand Iveton, who was executed in 1957 for placing a bomb in the factory where he worked. The bomb did not explode—because his goal was not to kill but he attracted attention to the issue of fighting colonialism. After independence, a street was named for him in the former Jewish neighborhood, but a year ago, the municipality of Oran removed Iveton's name and replaced it with that of another martyr. Citizens protested this decision, especially people from the neighborhood, so the municipality gave in and returned Iveton to his rightful place, adding the word "martyr" to his name.

Soltani recalled a similar story about Jean-Marie Larribère, whose name graces the street where his office was located. Larribère came to Algeria with his family in 1898 when he was five. He was a teacher before deciding to study medicine and was the first to introduce the Lamaze Method in Algeria in the 1950s. The mothers of Oran used to venerate him. He was a member of the Algerian Communist Party and a supporter of Algeria's liberation. His five daughters were all freedom fighters who were either imprisoned or expelled by the colonial authorities. Fighters belonging to the Organisation Armée Secrète (OAS) attempted to kill Dr. Larribère many times but without success, so they set out to blow up the clinic he had built in the 1950s, which was given to the Algerian state after independence. In the early '90s, the clinic was named after him, but a year ago, something strange happened. The municipality of Oran decided to remove his name and replace it with that of a native Muslim Algerian freedom fighter. Civil society activists and members of his family successfully led a massive media campaign to push the local authorities to reverse their decision, and the street carries his name to this day.

As soon as he got to the office, Colonel Soltani called his aides to come meet him. Derraji arrived first, followed by Ziane, who was carrying his papers. Captain Ziane was not a patient man and was not in the habit of waiting his turn to speak, so he launched right into it, laying out the information he had gathered on Hoopoe from his special sources: Sabri had participated in an active guerrilla group in Oran and managed to save himself by fleeing to Morocco. There he joined the entourage of Abdelhafid Boussouf and began his career in intelligence work, gathering files and information that he used to his advantage following independence. He was an expert in scaring his enemies and threatening them by using confidential information against them. Sometimes he would issue veiled threats in the guise of offering advice. People say he once requested an appointment with a customs official who was causing delays for some of his business interests. When they met, he did not directly discuss his problem. Instead, he advised the employee to be sure to keep an eye on his oldest daughter, a student at the Sorbonne University in Paris who, Sabri told him, had had an abortion two weeks prior after becoming pregnant by a French classmate. A scandal such as this—were people to learn of it—would destroy the father's reputation forever! A week later, the employee invited him to lunch, thanked him for letting him know about his daughter, and told him more than once that he was at his service any time. As for his famous nickname, "Hoopoe," there was more than one version of the story. Some say it goes back to when he started his guerrilla work carrying messages between the soldiers. He was like the hoopoe mentioned in the Qur'an, that acted as a messenger between the Prophet Solomon and the Queen of Sheba. Others said that his enemies came up with the nickname after independence, complaining about his cunning use of information for blackmail and other maneuvering.

Soltani emphasized that the assigned task for their team boiled down to shining light on the nature of the crime. In other words, determining whether or not it should be considered a terrorist act. And if it became clear that the motive had no connection to terrorism, they would hand the case over to the police. As for the investigation into Hoopoe's fortune and its sources, that fell under the auspices of the Accounts Board, which was authorized to investigate sources of wealth and prosecute bribe-takers and embezzlers.

"Do you have any information about the villa, Derraji?" asked the Colonel.

"It belongs to Hoopoe, sir."

"The widow denied knowing anything about it."

"Perhaps she was telling the truth. The deceased was a huge whoremonger."

Ziane could not contain himself and broke out laughing, which caused the others to laugh as well. Derraji used the word "whoremonger" not just to refer to someone who frequents prostitutes, but also to refer to someone who is shrewd and wicked. She mentioned that she had asked the neighbors about the previous night, tossing out questions without revealing any details of the crime, and noted what the guard of the villa across the street told her. He had seen a car enter the garage of the deceased's villa at around 1:30 a.m., when he heard a man's voice.

"Get in there, bitch!"

A woman was following him, laughing as she said, "Shame on you, sir."

Derraji confirmed that Hoopoe's personality was not free of contradictions. Yes, he loved women and gambling, but he would not let the opportunity pass to make the pilgrimage to God's house in Mecca. Then she spoke about his two daughters. The first one, Mona, was a physics professor at the University of Oran. She was married to a former Islamist named Badrou Bouzar. The second one, Souad, was killed during the years of terrorism in the '90s. People say that Hoopoe was the target, but he got away, and his daughter paid the price.

After listening to what his two aides had to say, the Colonel told them about his meeting with Hoopoe's widow. He lingered on an analysis of her personality and touched upon the guerrilla group and its four members. Until then, there had been some ambiguity surrounding the fourth member, Abbas Badi, aka Stork. He might be the thread that would lead to the truth. What happened to him? Did he betray his comrades?

When the meeting was done, as the Colonel was urging his aides to keep at it, his cell phone rang. It was General Belkacemi wanting to go over the latest developments. This case was critical. It could affect his reputation and stand in the way of his promotion. He asked the Colonel how the meeting with the widow went, and Soltani told him it had been helpful. Then he laid out the principal theory: The crime involved a settling of accounts that went back to the War of Independence. The General asked him to go meet with the deceased's son-in-law, Badrou Bouzar, who had been taken to a private clinic after fainting at the scene of the crime that morning. He gave him the clinic's address and told him that Badrou would be expecting him. It was not usual for the Boss to arrange meetings for the Colonel, but the pressure being applied to him from the higher-ups was having an effect and made him act like an energetic secretary.

Colonel Soltani asked himself one question: What was Badrou Bouzar doing at the crime scene at 6 a.m. on Independence Day?

4

Summer 1962

Miloud Sabri, aka Hoopoe, Zahra Misbah, aka Dolores, Abbas Badi, aka Stork, and Driss Talbi, aka Falcon, reunited in Medina Jedida a month before the referendum on independence. Their meeting was filled with excitement for the future. They were overjoyed that Falcon had been spared the guillotine and was released from prison after de Gaulle's general amnesty for people in prison and on death row. They stayed up all night. Dolores talked about her adventures in the mountains, where she had become a skilled nurse after spending time with doctors, nurses, and surgeons. She learned from harsh experience how to make do with what was available. Numerous times, she had to stand in for the doctor to pull a tooth, remove a bullet, or amputate a hand or leg to save someone's life. Hoopoe was reluctant to go into too much detail about his work in the intelligence service. Instead of spying on enemies and their agents, he was assigned to spy on the

Algerian freedom fighters, which also extended to monitoring the general Algerian population. And the truth was, he did not fall short. He carried out orders with extreme professionalism and great pleasure.

They looked different. Stork and Dolores seemed to have lost weight and were somewhat pale. They had tasted the bitterness of hunger and blockade, as had Liberation Army soldiers inside the country. Falcon had not fared any better than them, as prison and awaiting the guillotine never helped anyone stay healthy. Nevertheless, he did not lose his playful spirit; he said with a smile to Hoopoe, "I see life in Morocco has agreed with you."

"Morocco's amazing, brother."

"Had the food been a little less plentiful, it would have been better for you," quipped Stork.

"You know me, brother. I can't resist Moroccan sweets!"

They all laughed, and the three comrades remarked on Hoopoe's weight gain, as well as on the Moroccan accent he had picked up, using Moroccanisms such as *mizyan* for "amazing," *wakha* for "okay," and *daba* for "now." Stork became serious again, describing the miserable conditions that had befallen the Liberation Army inside the national territory of Algeria due to a lack of supplies and equipment. This was in contrast to the Border Army and both the armed and political forces that stood by watching and arguing among themselves, availing themselves of the good life abroad. Hoopoe realized the criticism was partially directed at him. He tried to soothe things with a bit of diplomacy, saying, "Every revolution makes mistakes."

"And everyone who makes a mistake must be held accountable," added Stork.

"We need to think about the future, not the past," responded Hoopoe.

Despite their differences, they all agreed the Revolution was a beginning, not an end. The challenges that came with independence were significant, the most basic of which was building a strong country on solid foundations. They discussed how a country should embrace a great revolution, about the sort of country they dreamed of, and where the Europeans fit in. Falcon criticized Ahmed Ben Bella's famous declaration: "We are Arabs. We are Arabs. We are Arabs. We are Arabs!"

"A leader like him should have envisioned a future Algeria large enough for Arabs, Chaouis, Kabyles, Tuaregs, and Mzabis. And why not Europeans too? Why build a new country based on exclusion?"

"I'm not convinced, Falcon. Europeans think of Algeria as their own private plantation," Dolores commented.

"And we'll always be the servants," added Stork.

"One thing I'm sure of is that we need to be wary of them. They'll do everything in their power to ensure the failure of the Revolution and independence," Hoopoe said sternly.

They spent some time on two questions: Would the National Liberation Army remain in the barracks once independence was achieved? And would the political organizations that existed just before the start of the war on November 1, 1954, return? Hoopoe tried to convince them that the National Liberation Front Party and Army were two significant pluses. There was no need to renounce them. During the war, they played a pivotal role in uniting the ranks and would play an even more substantial role in building the country's foundations. Falcon was not so sure. He stressed that relying on a single party and including the army in politics were two paths to a monopolization of power, suppressing freedoms, persecuting opponents, and strangling the young state in the cradle. As examples, he cited the Egyptian experience with Gamal Abdel Nasser and some other communist countries around the world.

"Falling into the trap of dictatorship is an imminent danger," said Falcon.

Stork, Falcon, and Hoopoe had not forgotten their history teacher, so they headed to his apartment in Plateau Saint-Michel. Professeur Rondeau was overjoyed to see them safe after four years had passed. He seemed to have aged prematurely and told them about the difficulties he had endured, which included having divorced his wife, Madelaine, after she became an active member of the OAS; she was able to save her skin and flee to Spain. Then he glanced at a frame that contained a large picture of Albert Camus, who had met his fate in a car accident in January 1960, and said in a sad voice, "Camus was wrong when he said we're condemned to live here. Divorce is just as good an option for groups as for individuals. In fact, it can keep one brother from killing the other. This land is soaked with the blood of brothers. Bravo, Cain!"

The teacher also affirmed his miscalculation concerning General de Gaulle, who dealt with the Algerian situation from a political, rather than a military, perspective. He was convinced that independence was inevitable, even though he understood that the medicine needed to be given in doses. In the beginning, during his first visit to Algeria in 1958, he reassured everyone with his famous statement: "*Je vous ai compris.* I understand you." Then, gradually, he proceeded to present such solutions as integration, coexistence, brotherhood, and then, finally, self-rule and independence.

"Algeria was a heavy burden for General de Gaulle. He had to get rid of it," said Falcon.

"Not all of Algeria, though. He made every effort to hold on to the Algerian Sahara in the south," responded Hoopoe.

"True. Because the Algerian Sahara is useful for two reasons . . . ," said the teacher, waiting for the answer.

"Petroleum," said Stork.

"And continued nuclear experiments," added Falcon.

"Very good!" the teacher said as if they were still his students.

Of course, they could not avoid talking about the OAS, which was established at the start of 1961, and then proceeded to seek revenge on those who rejected the idea that Algeria should remain a part of France. Its goal was to create a state of general chaos in order to guarantee the failure of the Evian Accords, which had put a stop to the war. This chaos would then require the French army to get involved, but de Gaulle was determined to end the war and grant Algeria its independence.

Slander and revenge abounded amid a general atmosphere of terror. Death became familiar to the Oranians. Bodies were thrown into the streets. Killers aimed randomly and stupidly. OAS fighters even invented a deadly new game that would designate specific days for killing people with particular professions: one day for barbers, another for domestic servants, another for mailmen and newspaper vendors, and so on. During the month of Ramadan on February 28, 1962, there was a horrific slaughter in Tahtaha Square in Medina Jedida when a car bomb exploded, taking the lives of eighty people.

It was insane in Oran at that time. The specter of death loomed over the city. Terror reigned to the point where Europeans were encouraged to flee the city by air, land, or sea, and the process of appropriating their houses began.

"Do you intend to leave as well, Professeur?" asked Hoopoe.

"Where to? To the land of my forefathers in Alsace-Lorraine?! I'll stay here where I was born and... where I will die. The few times I've visited France, they made fun of me because of my French-Algerian accent. I won't give them another chance." He let out a booming laugh, which quickly spread to the three friends.

Hoopoe learned that his former boss, Bernard Clavel, had left for Paris with his family but was determined to return after things calmed down and security was established. It occurred to Hoopoe to take possession of the villa where he had worked as a gardener, which he did easily. He broke in early one morning and spent his first night in the most beautiful room there was. He could not believe that his dream had become a reality. Subsequently, he employed his expertise from the intelligence services to propagate rumors regarding Clavel's supposed connection to the OAS. Hoopoe was sure he would never return to Oran. With that, the villa became his, and no one challenged him on it. His father was not happy, though, and said angrily, "Seizing people's property is forbidden. Haram."

"Then why did we take up the fight for independence? For things to stay as they were?" Hoopoe scoffed.

His father did not say another word.

As the referendum on independence—set for July 1, 1962—approached, the pace of OAS operations picked up with the targeting of civilian and military supporters of General de Gaulle. This situation resulted in a new alliance between the French powers that supported Algeria's independence and the Liberation Front, all to eliminate a common enemy. Within the framework of this security and intelligence cooperation, Hoopoe met a French officer who had taken part in the 1958 arrest of Yazid, Hoopoe and his three companions' superior. After his third glass, the officer would forget the world and everything in it, which is how Hoopoe learned who was behind Yazid's betrayal. Miloud convinced the officer to let him look at the entire file himself. Then he took advantage of the chaos surrounding the transfer of archives to France to steal the file. He was sure he had obtained a priceless treasure, so he held on to it.

Stork came forward to propose to Dolores, and her father consented. After a month, the marriage agreement was completed. Why wait any longer?

The imam repeated, "The sooner, the better," after reciting the opening verses of the Qur'an.

They were happy and began to plan for the future with great optimism. Dolores busied herself preparing for the wedding in record time. Usually, wedding preparations took a full year. She received help from her older sister, Farida, as well as some other relatives and friends.

But a week before the wedding reception, Falcon phoned Hoopoe, Dolores, and Stork and asked that they come to his new apartment in Sidi Houari immediately. He refused to say why, no matter how much they insisted. They arrived within minutes of one another and did not expect to hear a piece of news that would turn their lives upside down. Falcon stared at Stork and said, "You need to get out of here."

"Why?"

"The Liberation Front has sentenced you to death," Falcon replied nervously.

"Be kind to us, oh gentle Lord!" said Dolores, putting her shaking right hand over her mouth.

"Do they have proof?" asked Hoopoe.

Falcon had learned from a close friend who had been with him in prison that Stork was accused of working as an enemy agent and betraying Yazid, their superior, four years earlier. Omar swore to avenge his betrayed cousin.

Stork assured everyone he was prepared to turn himself in immediately and face his accusers, but his three comrades tried to convince him to wait. It was well known that Omar was a bloodthirsty man who knew nothing of diplomacy. After some back-and-forth, they agreed that Stork would temporarily hide in an empty apartment vacated by some Europeans in Saint-Eugène until the storm passed. The three sought help from some intermediaries to calm the situation and find a solution.

Attempts at mediation failed because Omar, who was personally leading the search campaign, made it a condition that Stork surrender himself first. He had not been hiding for more than two days before they figured out where he was. He could not believe his eyes when he saw Omar and his men charge into the bedroom at dawn, bristling with weapons. They had managed to enter through the kitchen window. They drove him to a villa in Canastel, and Omar himself took charge of the interrogation, then the torture. Stork's attempts at convincing the torturers of his innocence were futile, but they were unsuccessful in getting him to confess, so Omar ordered his men to tie him up by the neck like a sheep. Then he reached into his inside pocket and pulled out a Bousaâdi dagger. Stork was sure his time had come, so he proceeded to recite the Shahada, the Muslim profession of faith, and repeated the beginning of the freedom fighters' anthem:

From our mountains, the voice of the free rises up
Calling us to independence,
Calling us to the independence of our country.

Omar was outraged. He perceived it as a provocation and a deep insult to the martyrs. In his fury, he kicked him as he yelled, "Death is not enough for you, you bastard!"

"Oh my country, my country, I only love you," Stork continued to sing in a hoarse voice.

"You'll regret it for the rest of your life, you traitor!"

"Oh my country, my country..."

Stork saw the Bousaâdi come closer and closer, and he gulped, closing his eyes. He did not feel the pain in his neck, but rather, in his nose. He felt the blood gush over his lips. He opened his mouth to breathe and almost vomited, so strong was the taste of blood. He took a weak breath and passed out.

He regained consciousness at sunset and found himself having been thrown into the street. The pain was overwhelming, like nothing he had ever felt before. He tried to get up on his feet but could not. He closed his eyes again. He wanted to convince himself that what had happened was just a nightmare, nothing more. Maybe after a few moments, he would wake up from his slumber, curse Satan, and seek help from God. He opened his eyes to the sound of footsteps and saw a man and a woman approaching. He heard them speaking French and understood that the man did not want any trouble or to get involved in matters that did not concern them. The woman wanted to help. After a bit of back-and-forth, the man gave in. They helped Stork up and took him to a nearby house.

Stork received first aid and found sufficient care from the Febvres. He was lucky because Monsieur Febvre was a doctor and was able to stop the bleeding. The French woman did not stop insulting General de Gaulle, who had gone back on his promise of keeping Algeria French and who had betrayed the Europeans and their noble Muslim allies. The way the Febvres saw it, Stork was a Harki soldier who fought for France, and members of the Liberation Front had taken revenge on him by cutting off his nose. Stork decided to go along with it and not tell them the truth.

He remained in the Febvres' home for five days. That whole time, he thought about how to escape this horrible situation. He mulled over several scenarios, including suicide. The nose is the symbol of honor, and it was gone. How could he restore it? Who would believe he was innocent? He thought about his beloved Dolores, which caused his tears to flow. He swore never to show his face to her. Death would be better than for her to look at him and his...his severed nose and lost honor. He could not bear her looking at him and could never accept her compassion. "But does Dolores really believe I would betray Yazid?" he asked himself.

One evening, as a joke, Monsieur Febvre suggested that the only solution for Stork, if he wanted to live among people without a nose, would be to join the Tuaregs, who live in the desert and cover the bottom half of their faces. Monsieur Febvre left the sitting room for a few minutes and returned wearing Tuareg clothing he had bought from a merchant in Marché de la Bastille. His wife laughed, and Stork's smile returned to him for the first time in days.

The following day, after Monsieur Febvre and his wife went out to the market, Stork took the opportunity to leave. When they came home, he was gone. They rushed to see if anything had been stolen and breathed a sigh of relief when they were assured the jewelry and money were safe. Then they asked themselves: Why did he leave without saying goodbye? Why didn't he steal anything? Had they come back to finish him off?

Abbas Badi, aka Stork, left the city of his birth with tears running down his cheeks. He was overwhelmed by a terrible feeling that he would end up living far from it and in total isolation. As he wiped away his tears, he imagined himself sitting in one of the cafés in Tahtaha listening to his favorite singer, Ahmed Wahbi, sing:

Oran... Oran, you went to hell.
The smart ones ran away from you.
They sit confused in exile,
An exile that's treacherous and hard.

Hoopoe, Dolores, and Falcon were baffled when they searched the apartment where Stork had been hiding. He was nowhere to be found. He had disappeared without a trace. The apartment was as they had left it the day before. Why did he disappear? Where did he go? Did he run away? Was he truly a traitor?

They searched everywhere for him but found nothing. It was as if he were salt that had dissolved into hot soup. Then they became even more baffled and nervous when each received a postcard, sent to their new addresses. The cards were identical. "One of you is next."

The three comrades spent long hours discussing the postcard from every angle. They recalled guerrilla operations they had been a part of and laid out a number of scenarios: Did Omar, Yazid's cousin, send the cards? But Omar was killed in a car accident a month after Stork's disappearance. Perhaps it was one of his men. If this were the case, the accusation of treason would not only be leveled at Stork, but at all of them as well. They stopped on an important point: The sender knew their new addresses. Were they under surveillance? What was the purpose of sending the card? Was it to threaten them? Why just threaten them? And what was preventing the threat from being carried out? Was it from someone who wanted to put them on edge or to avenge himself? But of what? Who was waiting to ambush them? Had Stork fallen victim to a conspiracy? Had they done away with him for good? And what if Stork himself had sent the cards? All these questions exhausted them.

"We must remain united," said Falcon.

"They'll kill us one by one," said Dolores, fighting back tears.

Hoopoe moved closer to her and said, "Don't be afraid, Dolores. I would give my life for you."

Dolores did not celebrate the joy of independence like all the other Algerians because of two major calamities: Stork had disappeared, and the wedding celebration had been canceled. This depressed her and led to a feeling of total isolation. What made matters worse was finding out that her dear neighbor, Pablo Garcia Mendez, had been killed. He was one of hundreds of Europeans, most of them innocent, who were killed on the 5th of July, Independence Day.

Abbas Badi, aka Stork, headed south to Tamanrasset, seeking refuge with one of his father's friends, Mabrouk Agh Hassani, a Tuareg merchant. Stork told him his story from beginning to end, to which Mabrouk responded, "Your secret is safe with me."

Agh Hassani eased Stork's integration into Tuareg society. He publicly declared that Stork was the son of his sister, who had lived and died in Oran. That was how Stork hid the truth and his severed nose. He began to earn a living thanks to his skill at dyeing. News reached him about Ahmed Ben Bella and the Border Army, led by Colonel Houari Boumediene, storming the capital of Algiers, and about the Algerians they killed. That is when the people spoke up.

"Seven years is enough!"

True, seven years was enough. Algerians were tired of war and wanted to benefit from a modicum of peace. During the Revolution, Stork witnessed the conflicts between states and the escalating power struggles within the ranks of Liberation Army officers. Each one wanted to impose his opinions on the others. He concluded that Algeria was like a ship in need of a captain who would steer it to safe harbor.

Stork secretly returned to Oran at the end of the summer to comfort his ailing mother, who had become ill out of worry for him. She wept when she saw what had happened to her son. He learned from her that his disappearance had caused a lot of talk in Medina Jedida. Rumors spread like wildfire, the most significant of which was that he had fled with the French army after his treachery had been discovered. Dolores's father publicly announced that the engagement was annulled and thanked God, who had saved him from a relationship through marriage with such a detestable traitor. And he repeated for everyone to hear, "That's that. Not another word."

Stork decided to observe the situation from up close. He was obsessed with what had happened to him, searching his memory for answers. He kept picturing Omar and his men breaking into his hiding spot. The only individuals who knew its location were his three companions. He insistently and angrily asked himself, "Who pointed them to where I was hiding? Is the person who betrayed me the same person who betrayed Yazid before that? Did all three of my comrades conspire against me? Was it two of them or just one who plotted against me? And if that's the case, what was the motive?"

He swore he would exact the most ruthless revenge on whoever had betrayed him.

5

Thursday, July 5, 2018

11:16 A.M.

Colonel Karim Soltani's cell phone rang. He kept driving with his left hand while reaching over to answer the call with his right. He saw the name Nadia—his ex-wife—on the screen. "God help me," he muttered to himself.

"Did you forget?" she snapped at him without any preamble.

"What?"

"Don't you remember?"

"Nadia, for God's sake, I don't have time to listen to your riddles."

"Didn't you promise your son you'd go with him to Mostaganem to visit his friend at ten this morning?"

"I can't. I'm swamped."

"Mostaganem isn't that far. Just an hour."

"I told you, I'm swamped."

"Busy even on Independence Day?!"

"For crying out loud!"

"Why don't you tell the truth? You want to spend the day with your mistress. You're a father in name only, sir!"

The Colonel hung up to limit the damage. He realized she was skillfully luring him into a war of words he would undoubtedly lose. Nadia was well-practiced at making the compelling case that he was a failed father and a failed husband. He had genuinely forgotten about Mostaganem. He expected his relationship with his son would suffer as a result and his ex-wife would pour more fuel on the fire. His cell phone rang again. He thought Nadia might be calling back to empty her quiver of poisonous words into him, but he was wrong. It was his aide, Captain Samir Ziane.

"We've caught a fish, sir."

"Welcome news."

"The fish is from Libya."

"Ah, Libyan fish, the tastiest of all."

Ziane had pored over the top-secret file on Hoopoe's connections to a terrorist group in Libya. After the fall of Qaddafi's regime, the deceased had started to spin a web of connections. He managed to gain the sympathy of sheikhs from some tribes there by supplying them with weapons and using a charitable organization as legal cover for his activities. Libya was not the end goal, though; it was a gateway to the other countries around it, including Tunisia, Egypt, Mali, and Niger.

Soltani urged his aide to continue investigating. After that, he called General Belkacemi and apprised him of the Libyan theory.

"So Hoopoe was killed by foreign entities?!" exclaimed the General.

"Too early to tell. It's just a theory, sir."

"But it's a good theory, Soltani."

After he hung up, the Colonel thought about how General Belkacemi seemed a little too enthusiastic about the Libyan theory. His primary impulse seemed to be to close the case as soon as possible to avoid pressure from the higher-ups. Soltani called his lover, but she didn't pick up. He knew she was still angry with him.

Soltani tore through the Colonel Lotfi neighborhood but couldn't find the clinic where Badrou Bouzar was. Finally, he got up the nerve to ask someone walking by who pointed him in the right direction. Street and plaza names in Oran are incredibly chaotic. Sometimes, you'll be looking for a street that might have two or three different names. Some people still preferred to use names that hearken back to the colonial era, knowing full well that they often referred to French generals who had exterminated Algerians. They even changed Rue Captain Hamri (named for the martyred war hero) back to Rue General Ferradou (named after a French general who served during the early Algerian campaigns of colonization), which the residents of Gambetta preferred.

"Our poor street. Demoted from general to captain!" That's how a friend of his who still lived on this street put it before the name change.

Soltani returned to the main street, named after the city of Dubai. With its proliferation of towers, shopping centers, and hotels, Dubai had become an oppressive architectural model for Oran, and developers strove to market this model using all the means at their disposal. They were building skyscrapers without paying any attention to the restoration and preservation of historically important neighborhoods such as Sidi Houari. If building the actual Dubai had cost two trillion dollars and years of serious planning, what resources would be necessary to build a new Dubai in Oran? Not to mention the many streams flowing underneath the city, making the ground unsuitable for tall buildings. Nonetheless, constructing buildings as high as thirty stories was permitted.

The neighborhood of Colonel Lotfi was originally farmland that was built up to commemorate one of the most illustrious martyrs of the War of Independence. This development began at the start of the new millennium and consisted of five- to ten-story buildings that showed no regard for architectural or aesthetic sense. The rooms in the apartments were small, there were no balconies, and there wasn't a trace of green space that would provide a breath of fresh air for the residents. And finding parking there was impossible. However, the neighborhood became increasingly desirable after the opening of the luxury Meridian Hotel, which coincided with the ministerial meeting of the Gas Exporting Countries Forum in 2010. Restaurants and stores were everywhere, and the neighborhood became a destination, especially at night.

Soltani parked his car in front of the clinic, which seemed to have just been built. In the last few years, private clinics had sprung up like weeds while public hospitals were on the verge of collapse. The top medical specialists emigrated to France and Canada, as the rest waited for the opportunity to leave. Hospital equipment was outdated, and sometimes there were no available beds, forcing the poor patients to lie down on the floor. Oh, where have the days of free medical care gone? In the '60s, '70s, and '80s, a good share of the revenue from oil exports was spent on the needs of the people. Today, it's every man for himself. Big fish eat little fish.

Soltani presented himself to the person working at the information desk and told him he had an appointment with Badrou Bouzar. He was asked to sit down in the reception area and wait for someone to take him to the patient's room.

After a little while, Soltani saw a beautiful young woman wearing a hijab walking toward him, a warm smile on her face.

"I'm Amira Derbal, Mr. Bouzar's secretary."

"Pleased to meet you, madame."

"I haven't risen to the rank of 'madame' yet," she said, widening her smile.

"Excuse me, miss. This morning, I'm in a stupor."

"No problem, sir. I've been expecting you. Please follow me."

He walked behind her, admiring her beautifully seductive gait. She was good-looking, just his type. Medium-sized. Neither tall nor short. Neither fat nor thin. Miss Derbal pressed the button for the third floor as they entered the elevator. They exchanged glances and smiled in silence.

When they got to the room, the secretary knocked on the door twice and opened it without waiting for a response. Then she made way for the Colonel.

Badrou Bouzar was wearing blue pajamas and sitting on a chair facing the bed. He got up to welcome the Colonel and invited him to sit on the balcony overlooking a flower garden.

"How are you now, Mr. Bouzar?"

"I praise and thank God. 'Yet it may happen that you will hate a thing which is better for you.' God Almighty has spoken the truth. It was quite a shock, and my heart cannot take too much."

Soltani did not want the interview to take longer than necessary, so he got right to the point. "Tell me, what were you doing at the crime scene at six a.m.?"

"I received three calls, one right after the other, from Uncle Miloud's cell phone."

"At what time?"

"Five-thirty."

"And what did he say to you?"

"Nothing. He didn't speak at all. But right after that, I received a text message asking me to come immediately. When I arrived, I found the inner and outer gates unlocked. I called out to him, but there was no answer. I went upstairs and found him in his room. Murdered. Do you want to see the text message, sir?"

"Yes, I do."

Badrou reached into his right pocket and took out his cell phone. He opened and handed it to the Colonel, who glanced at it, then returned it to Badrou.

"Tell me, Mr. Bouzar, does the villa belong to the deceased?"

"Yes, sir."

"Madame Dolores…I mean, Zahra Misbah said she didn't know about it."

"There are some things that need to be kept hidden from wives," Badrou Bouzar said with a smile.

"What do you mean?" asked the Colonel, seeking further explanation as if he didn't understand what he meant.

"Uncle Miloud, may God have mercy on him, loved women."

"Was the deceased by himself last night?"

"There's no way Uncle Miloud was up late by himself."

"Who was he with?"

"God only knows, sir."

It was not at all difficult to get Badrou Bouzar talking. He started to tell a long story about his illustrious history with the deceased. Soltani soon realized that he was not speaking off the cuff. He had prepared himself for this interview like a professional actor does when preparing for an important role. He confirmed that he met him in the mid-'80s and that they had not parted ways since. He was like a father and then some. Badrou described the deceased as one of the Revolution's heroes; one of its most distinguished figures. He gave his youth so that Algeria could enjoy freedom and well-being. After the fight for independence was won, he rolled up his sleeves and got to work building an independent Algeria.

Were they building Algeria or destroying it? Soltani was about to ask but refrained despite his many criticisms and reservations about what Badrou Bouzar had said. "Criticisms" was not quite the right word. Perhaps the word "questions" was more accurate. Questions such as: Were Algerians still happy living in a liberated Algeria? Were they ever? Why did most young people dream of leaving, risking their lives in deadly boats to get to the north shore of the Mediterranean? He didn't want to get into a long discussion as this wasn't the place for it. He had other priorities, and time was of the essence.

Soltani had heard enough about the deceased's laudable qualities and the heroic role he had played on behalf of the nation. It was time to get to the heart of the matter.

"You were close to the deceased, isn't that right, Mr. Bouzar?"

"Yes, it was my honor, sir."

"Who would have an interest in killing him?"

"Enemies of the nation."

"Who do you mean? Give me one name."

"The lawyer, Driss Talbi, who also goes by Falcon. Should I go on?"

"Please do."

"The political cartoonist, Rachid Kadri."

Badrou could not hide how much he hated Rachid Kadri. He accused Kadri of causing the murder of the deceased's youngest daughter in 1998. Hoopoe had asked the cartoonist to stay away from his daughter, but Rachid persisted in violating his honor. He never missed an opportunity to damage Hoopoe's reputation and denounce him publicly. He taunted him by inventing a character for his cartoons named "Brother Bandit." It was well known that the deceased often referred to people as "brother." Badrou emphasized that Rachid Kadri was lucky Hoopoe was a tolerant, big-hearted man. Had he wanted to hurt him, he would have beaten him senseless in the blink of an eye.

Driss Talbi, aka Falcon, did not escape Badrou Bouzar's barbs either. Badrou said that his animosity toward Hoopoe was not at all justified; most likely, this hatred went back to childhood. Falcon could not swallow the deceased's repeated successes and did everything he could to destroy him and besmirch his good name. There was a newspaper interview in which he attacked the deceased with slanders that could be considered defamatory, but Hoopoe categorically refused to seek refuge in the courts. He did not want to betray his trusted friends. Badrou added that he was in possession of a dossier that could destroy Falcon. In fact, he had asked his secretary just that morning to go to his office in the company headquarters and get a copy of it to hand over to investigators. Badrou turned toward the table, picked up a file folder, and handed it to the Colonel.

"Uncle Miloud did not deserve to die such an awful death. Those treacherous criminals cut his nose off on Independence Day so they could humiliate Algeria and those who fought for its freedom." As he said this, he unleashed his tears.

Soltani remained unaffected by crying, as he had seen Badrou cry earlier that morning at the crime scene. He had asked himself many times before why men's tears didn't affect him. Perhaps it was due to his general lack of confidence in men; he trusted women more, for sure. Over the course of his career, he had seen dangerous terrorist criminals crying like children, but he never felt sorry for them. In fact, it only increased his anger, hatred, and harshness toward them.

Soltani wanted to play his essential card, so he stood up and looked straight at Badrou as he asked, "Did the deceased have investments in Libya?"

"Libya?! What do you mean?" He acted shocked by the question.

"Meaning, did he have business there or not?"

"Yes, humanitarian business."

"More to the point, was he sending medicine or arms, Mr. Bouzar?"

"No. There was absolutely no connection between Uncle Miloud and arms or terrorism. He wanted the best for everyone, most of all for Muslims. Of course, the situation in our sister country, Libya, upset him. And he was scared it would become a failed state like Somalia, which might threaten Algeria's stability. He didn't have a personal stake in it. He wanted to help, for God's sake. And for the sake of our precious nation."

Having heard enough, he decided it was time to leave. He thanked Badrou and asked him not to leave Oran in case he might need him again. Badrou responded that he was always at his service and would do whatever was necessary to ensure the guilty party did not escape punishment.

"Whoever slaughtered Uncle Miloud and cut off his nose on Independence Day needs to pay dearly!"

When Soltani walked out of the room, he found the beautiful secretary sitting on one of the chairs in the hallway, waiting for him. She suggested walking him out, and he took her up on it. They walked together to the elevator. Secretaries, true to their titles, are keepers of secrets and sources of valuable information. However, he soon forgot all about the rules of the profession and Hoopoe's murder case as his eyes fixed on this girl walking two steps in front of him. He could smell her scent and was overwhelmed by an irresistible desire for her. Was she magnetic? He wondered if he should ask for her phone number. When the elevator door slid closed, the secretary broke the silence.

"May God rest Mr. Miloud's soul and console his family. He was exceptional in everything he did."

"How was his relationship with Mr. Bouzar?"

"Like father and son."

"Do you have any information about the deceased's investments in Libya?"

"I don't."

"Does Mr. Bouzar also invest in Libya?"

"I don't know, sir," she said, smiling.

He didn't insist on asking any more questions. When they reached the gate, he thanked the secretary for walking with him. He handed her his card and asked her to call if she remembered anything that might help with the investigation. She gave him her cell phone number, and he rushed to take it down. He thought he might call her after the Hoopoe case was done, and this idea pleased him.

He settled into the driver's seat of his car, and before starting the engine, he made three calls, one after the other. He started with his lover, Meriem. It rang and rang, but she didn't pick up. He gathered from this that the fires of anger were still smoldering. Then, he called his son, Malik, and got a busy signal. Finally, he tried calling the medical examiner, Abdou Hamlaoui, to try to expedite his report. He secured a promise that he would get him the autopsy results by late afternoon. Would he keep that promise? It isn't easy to ask someone to do twice the work on a day off, especially on Independence Day. It sure didn't feel like Independence Day!

After that, he called his aide, Malika Derraji, and tasked her with gathering as much information as she could on Rachid Kadri, the political cartoonist. For her part, Derraji informed him of the preliminary results of her review of the security cameras on the street where the love nest was located. The footage showed two people, their features indistinguishable, walking out of the villa's gate wearing tracksuits and caps.

"I have other information, sir."

"I'm listening."

First Lieutenant Derraji was able to reach the journalist who had published the investigation about Hoopoe's guerrilla group. He revealed a piece of information that he had been prevented from publishing. Every year on Independence Day, Hoopoe, Dolores, and Falcon received a postcard that said: "One of you is next."

"And who's sending them?" asked Soltani.

"The sender's identity is still unknown."

"It could be Abbas Badi, also known as Stork."

"A distinct possibility, sir."

"We need to focus on him. He might be the key to solving the puzzle of Hoopoe's murder."

6

Summer 1965

Zahra Misbah, aka Dolores, appeared in the most beautiful outfit: an Oranian blouse adorned with a gold arabesque. But she frowned despite the photographer repeating himself like a parrot.

"Smile, my girl. This is the happiest day of your life."

Ultimately, they stopped insisting and let her be, thinking that perhaps the reason was shyness. If only it were that! She was devastated over the loss of her first—and maybe last—love. Her sweetheart, Stork, was gone, and he had left questions behind that would poison that love.

"If he were truly innocent, why would he run away and disappear without a trace?! Oh, Abbas, Stork! You know what they say: 'What eye could ever bear again to see the lover who wounds the heart and makes it bleed?'"

As days went on, she came to believe in the betrayal theory, which had resulted in the arrest and killing under torture of their superior, Yazid Mansouri, in 1958.

Miloud Sabri, aka Hoopoe, asked Dolores to marry him, and she accepted. Annulling the previous engagement was a scandal, and popular wisdom dictated that scandals should be promptly addressed so that people would forget about them. Everyone admired Hoopoe, and many girls dreamed of marrying him. His ambitions were evident, and his future seemed prosperous in independent Algeria. She was sure Hoopoe loved her and was prepared to give his own life to protect her. She thought about it for a long time. She did not want to miss the marriage boat. She was twenty-four years old; her mother married when she was fifteen. As for her older sister, Farida, she had already gotten married and divorced twice and had not yet given up hope of finding a third husband.

Farida sought to convince her that love and marriage were like night and day; never the two shall meet. She also insisted that passion was a teenage sickness. It was possible to be cured of it in the mind, but not the heart. Perhaps her Aunt Saliha was right when she said marriage was like a runaway train. Sometimes, it stops, and other times it just keeps on going no matter who's waiting. You need to jump on and take the risk to get somewhere—anywhere—on that train. It doesn't matter where you end up, or whether sitting or standing. All that really matters is to avoid waiting too long and getting bored in the station. Dolores was aware of some basic truths, including that spinsterhood was a disaster in this cruel society. While she had run an elementary school in Sidi Houari since independence and really loved her work, professional success was not enough. A woman without a man was like a car without an engine. There was no way to move forward.

Celebratory trills burst out when Hoopoe sat next to his bride and reached his hands out to his mother so she could henna them. The voice of Blaoui Houari, one of Oran's stars, rose up, and those in attendance were dazzled by the most beautiful of his songs:

Listen... listen
My darling... listen.
Your beauty is captivating; I've never found anything like it in any other country.
My beautiful gazelle, my heart finds pleasure only in you.

Professeur Rondeau stole the spotlight with his dancing skills. Light and spontaneous on his feet, he combined traditional and modern dances. And keeping up with his every step was the bride's brother, Youssef Misbah, who had just returned from the Soviet Union, where he was part of a training delegation hosted by the KGB for officers in Military Security. Hoopoe could not have been happier. He had achieved a dream he thought was nearly impossible. Would Dolores share his feelings... someday? He told himself he would make her love him as much as he loved her. More, even. He was sure that Stork was the past and that *he* was the present and future. And what a difference there was between the past and the future. The past is death. The future is life.

Hoopoe threw himself fully into two games: amassing power and betting on horses. While working in intelligence during the war and fighting in the National Liberation Front Party ranks after the country gained its independence, he realized early on that true power is invisible. There were many political romantics like his lifelong friend, Driss Talbi, aka Falcon, who believed power needed to lie in the government, the parliament, or in the machinery of one party. But that was not how it worked in the real world. Discussion of the first constitution ratified after independence in 1963 was held by a handful of politicians loyal to President Ahmed Ben Bella in the Majestic Cinema movie theater in Bab El Oued in Algiers, far from the eyes of most elected members of parliament. Si Ahmed—or Brother Ben Bella as he liked people to call him—consolidated practically all the power for himself. He was President of the Republic, Prime Minister, Secretary General of the only existing party, and the Minister of the Interior, Finance, and Communications. He also strove to take control of the army by installing Colonel Tahar Zbiri as Army Chief of Staff and reducing the influence of his rival, the Minister of Defense, Houari Boumediene.

As for the second game—betting on horses—it had quickly become an addiction. He was convinced that wielding power was like betting on horses because both were based on risk. You win some, you lose some. A sense of failure was part of the game, and winning after failing was especially sweet because it was mixed with vengeance. Over time, he came to believe that power was the art of distinguishing between enemies and allies, or between crossbred and thoroughbred horses. By following horse races and observing the struggle between Ben Bella and Boumediene, he determined who the purebred horse was. Without hesitation, he bet on Boumediene because the final word always goes to the strongest, or the one with the weapons. People often said to him that Ben Bella enjoyed the people's support, to which he would laugh, "The people will support whoever is left standing. Everyone loves winners and hates losers, and Algerians are no exception. They're just like everyone else."

One day, in one of the cafés of Tahtaha, Hoopoe listened to a peasant give a lovely description of the people. He said they're like the woman who knows she's weak and will always need a courageous man to protect her. First and foremost, the people are looking for a strong leader under whose wing they can find protection. Hoopoe really liked this analogy and paid for the man's drinks as well as those of the people sitting at his table. Hoopoe remarked that comparing the people to a woman was not so different from the comparison he had come up with, that the people are like a horse. First, you need to break it in. Then you get up on it and ride it where you want to go. To which someone shouted out enthusiastically, "Our people are like a donkey . . . they need to be prodded with a stick." Everyone laughed.

Right before celebrating the third anniversary of independence—a Saturday—Falcon was in Hoopoe and Dolores's villa. They heard the news of a coup against the elected president, Ahmed Ben Bella, and the news was confirmed when Colonel Houari Boumediene's thin face and stern glasses looked out from the television to address those watching:

> Oh, proud Algerian people, your silence does not come out of fear or surrender to tyranny, as the tyrant who was removed from power today had thought. He thought you had given in to a deep sleep, but events have shown otherwise. They have taught that avenging those you love must align with how much you trust them and how sincere you are in your support for them. Otherwise, they will deviate from the right path or betray the trust that has been placed in their hands.
>
> The Revolutionary Council will work to create the conditions necessary to establish a serious democratic country governed by laws that respect morals and ideals. A country that does not disappear with any given government or individual.

Hoopoe welcomed the Revolutionary Council, and having bet on the winning side, he was happy with the coup. Dolores supported the change because the country needed a tough leader, and the struggles of those who had governed Algeria's six states following independence were still fresh in people's minds. The disagreements between Ben Bella and Boumediene were visible to all. Falcon's reaction was not the same as theirs, and he laid out his opposition to the coup.

"Despite his many shortcomings, Ben Bella remains a representative of the people. He came to the presidency by way of the ballot box. And what about the elected parliament? What's the justification for dissolving parliament along with other standing institutions and suspending the constitution? It would be better to fix what's already there rather than destroy the whole thing. That will just create a dangerous vacuum and push the country toward the unknown."

"Change is inevitable, brother," said Hoopoe enthusiastically.

"Revolutionary redress is a military dictatorship."

"Why all this pessimism, brother?"

"I'm a realist."

"The Revolution is sick and needs medicine."

"There's no sickness and no treatment. Nothing of the sort. The Revolution and the people are fine," exclaimed Falcon.

"The people need a strong leader, brother."

"The problem isn't with the people. It's with those in power."

Falcon explained his opposition to ascending to power on top of tanks. No country can flourish and enjoy stability when the military gets involved in politics. Military coups, by their very nature, demolish all plans to build a cohesive country. He cited the example of Syria, which witnessed four bloody military coups in just two years between 1949 and 1951. The revolutionary redress that Colonel Boumediene was calling for was a smoke screen. His goal was not to protect the Revolution and defend the interests of the people. Rather, it was to grab the reins of power and eliminate his rival, Ben Bella. Falcon also said that he was uncomfortable with the Colonel for another reason that was connected to his nom de guerre, Houari Boumediene. It wasn't that he had gotten rid of his real name, Mohammed Boukherouba. Rather, it was that he incorporated the names of two righteous saints, Sidi Houari and Sidi Boumediene, and made them his own.

"Does he want Algerians to sanctify him? Is he striving to be a ruler or a saint? Does he want to make Algeria a country that doesn't fade away as men do, as he says, or a Sufi *zaouia* for pilgrims and seekers of baraka and blessings from the righteous? Why mix religion and politics?" fumed Falcon.

Following independence, Falcon entered university to fulfill his dream of becoming a lawyer. He went out with Dolores's older sister, Farida, numerous times. Their relationship developed, and they decided to marry, which was done quickly and made Dolores very happy. She was convinced that the marriage would help Falcon and Hoopoe move beyond their deep political differences. One day, Zahra proposed passing a law that basically prohibited discussing politics at the table. Farida strongly supported her sister's suggestion, but its implementation failed miserably. For Falcon and Hoopoe, political debate came as naturally as breathing. They were like two fighting cocks that would never stop going at one another. Their discussions were heated, punctuated by verbal attacks that used harsh-sounding words circulating at the time such as "reactionary," "labor," "empire," "exploitation of the masses," "betrayal of the Revolution," and "martyrs." And then there were other words to counter them, such as "political naïveté," "people are like horses," and "balance of power." But in the end, every time they would hug, and one would say to the other, "May God guide you!"

The disappearance of Abbas Badi, aka Stork, after being accused of betraying their superior Yazid during the war in 1962 kept Falcon up at night. He must have left some trace. There was no way he could just melt away like a sugar cube in hot tea. Indeed, he was right. As he flipped through a French weekly magazine dedicated to the third anniversary of Algeria's independence, a French woman's account caught his attention. Her last name was Febvre. Born and raised in Oran, she left after independence and settled in Lyon, France. She told the story of a young Algerian man who had stood with the French and paid the ultimate price when the Liberation Front exacted savage revenge by cutting off his nose. She mentioned that this had occurred in the summer of 1962. She went into great detail describing the poor young man and his misfortune. Falcon's curiosity was piqued. He wanted more details, so he called up the French magazine and asked to speak with the journalist who had written up the French woman's story. After trying for two days, he was able to get in touch with the journalist. He made up a story that Madame Febvre was a relative of his and that he had lost touch with her family after the mass exodus from Algeria in the summer of 1962. The journalist was sympathetic and gave him the woman's phone number.

Falcon called Madame Febvre immediately, doing away with the initial story and coming up with another tearjerker. He told her he was looking for his sister who had helped the French and disappeared without a trace right before the referendum for independence. He didn't need to expend too much effort for her to open up. Madame Febvre could have competed with the best chitchatters in the world, and he let her talk to her heart's delight so he could gather as much information as possible. She cursed General de Gaulle in the strongest terms and described him as the most vile traitor. She told the story of the poor young man from beginning to end, providing some commentary of her own. She mentioned that her husband was still convinced it was the young man who had stolen the Tuareg clothes he was so fond of. The physical description—height, eye and hair color—matched Stork's. When she started to repeat herself, he cut her off.

"Do you remember the young man's name, Madame Febvre?"

"Of course I do. I could never forget it."

"What was it?"

"Abbas."

Falcon thanked her for the information. He felt an overwhelming joy but held off telling Hoopoe and Dolores. That same day, he visited Stork's mother and delivered the good news that her son was not dead and that he would do everything he could to find him. She wished him all the best, as she always did, but did not cry for joy, nor did she ululate in celebration. Her reaction gave him some pause. She was not gladdened by the news; it was as if she knew he was alive and being cared for. But how did she know? She was likely to be secretive about such important things. Then he thought of something he hadn't before. If Stork were still alive, he would never abandon his mother. During the War of Independence, he took great risks, coming down from the mountains and sneaking into Medina Jedida to see her. Stork was a master of camouflage.

Driss Talbi lived up to his nickname, "Falcon," and he was not satisfied with mere verbal opposition to the new regime. He joined a secret group of militants, the majority of whom were leftists, and formed a cell to resist Boumediene's coup. After less than two weeks, though, the security apparatuses discovered it through leaks that had existed from the beginning, and they were arrested. Falcon got a taste of torture in a free Algeria that was much worse than what he had experienced under the French. The one who supervised his torture was a veteran freedom fighter nicknamed "The Burnt," so called because he had been tortured horribly by French soldiers; half of his body was burned. This experience confirmed for Falcon what the French inspector who had interrogated him in 1958 had said about victims imitating their torturers. Before his trial, Falcon was sent back to the Casbah prison, where he had spent four years waiting for his death sentence to be carried out during the Revolution.

Hoopoe did everything in his power to help Falcon, but none of his many connections succeeded in securing his release. Hoopoe and Dolores stood by his wife, Farida, and took care of all the lawyers' fees, and Falcon thanked them for their generosity and loyalty when they visited him in prison. He was angrier at President Boumediene than he had ever been, saying, "The only positive thing to come out of the June 19, 1965, coup is that the military has come to rule out in the open rather than behind the scenes."

In the meantime, Abbas Badi, aka Stork, secretly visited his mother in Medina Jedida. He came to her at sundown wrapped in a traditional women's haik. That night, he heard sad news from her. Dolores had married his friend, Hoopoe. As for his other friend, he had been arrested and was sitting in prison—the same one the colonial authorities had put him in as he awaited his death sentence to be carried out. Was the dream of love and independence lost? Had the dream turned into a nightmare? Had the new rulers turned into neocolonizers? These questions floated around in his head, but he did not want to think about them.

Stork did not say a word about this news. He was broken up with pain and sadness. Eventually, he had heard enough and started to cry in his mother's arms without shame, like he did when he was a little boy.

Thursday, July 5, 2018

12:25 P.M.

"Sidi Houari is dying, people," Colonel Karim Soltani repeatedly sighed whenever he set foot in this ancient neighborhood. Some of the buildings were in ruins, while others were on the verge of collapse. Someone who didn't know its history would think they were looking at the aftermath of an air *and* land bombardment. Most of its inhabitants were relocated to other neighborhoods in the medina, while a stalwart few refused to leave. In recent years, African migrants found what they were looking for in the abandoned dwellings. As Sidi Houari resisted death, opposing voices rose up, some calling for the restoration and preservation of the neighborhood's heritage and others calling for tearing it down and following Dubai Marina's lead.

Soltani went up the building's stairs. Being careful not to trip on the scattered holes, he safely reached the second floor. He rang the bell and a woman in her seventies opened the door for him. He introduced himself and asked if he could see the lawyer Driss Talbi, aka Falcon, about an urgent matter. She did not ask if he had an appointment. She just welcomed him and smiled, "I'm the lawyer's wife, and his secretary when needed. Please, follow me."

She walked with him to the reception area, and he found himself in a small room with space enough for six chairs around a small round table scattered with old newspapers and magazines. He glanced at four posters on the walls of revolutionary martyrs: Larbi Ben M'hidi, Hassiba Ben Bouali, Amirouche, and Ahmed Zabana. He was surprised that Falcon also worked on holidays. There was an old woman in her eighties waiting her turn. She told Soltani that the lawyer helped those who needed it. If not for his goodness and generosity, many would live permanently oppressed and without justice in this country.

"In this country, there's equal justice for the poor man, but not for everyone, my son."

He cracked a smile tinged with sorrow because this sort of discontent touched his honor as a representative of an essential state institution. The old woman told him that her husband was bedridden because of a chronic illness and that her second son was killed in the mid-'90s. He did not want to embarrass her with uncomfortable questions such as: Who killed him? How was he killed? Was he butchered with a knife, or was he shot? Did he die under torture? Which division did he fight in? Was he with the state or against it?

The proverb "Keep the well covered" played on repeat in his head. What was the use of so many questions when answers were so scarce? The wounds of those years were still prominent on his skin and in his memory. Soltani had faced three assassination attempts, and the scar on his right thigh attested to the bullet that had torn his flesh. As for his wounded memory, it also was still painfully raw as a result of the assassinations of so many people he loved. This included his father, who was slaughtered like an Eid sheep as an example to others, all because he stood up to terrorists. And what was there to say about his close friend and colleague, Nourredine? Betrayed and killed right in front of him as he watched helplessly. As he held him in his arms, his life left him while he repeated, "They betrayed me, Karim, my brother!"

Who betrayed him? And why? Sometimes the painful memories came back without any warning and floated up to the surface. How deadly those years were when death waited for him at every moment. He was in his twenties, or as they say in the language of poets, "he was in the age of flowers," but in reality, they were the absolute worst years of his life. That is why he hated hearing El Hachemi Guerouabi's song "Yesterday, When I Was Twenty." He could not stand nostalgic tunes.

He spent that period steeped in alcohol to help him forget and lighten the weight of fear and anxiety. His journey into the hell of addiction lasted a full year, during which he almost wrecked and lost everything. He started to drink more and more following the assassination of his friend Noureddine. One night, after two drinks, he went to the bathroom. While washing his hands, he looked in the mirror and saw a face he barely recognized. He hung his head low and wept deeply for himself. Then he stared into the mirror again. He dried his tears and washed his face. At that moment, he decided not to continue down that road. He went back to the living room, grabbed the bottle of wine, and returned to the bathroom, where he poured the rest of the bottle down the toilet. The red wine mixed with the urine. That night was a turning point for him. After that, he sought balance and focused on his health and work. Moreover, he made the most of his time to pursue his hobby of learning foreign languages. He mastered English, which he had studied at university, and added Spanish as well.

During that period, nighttime was difficult for him. He could not sleep unless the darkness cleared. He tried all the sleeping pills there were, but they didn't work. Doctors were baffled as to what he was suffering from, and, in the end, they told him his problem was psychological, not physical. They advised him to change his lifestyle for the sake of his health, but this meant quitting his job in Anti-Terrorism and abandoning the front lines in the midst of the battle like a deserter. It would be a betrayal of the trust that had been placed in him. His father, the betrayed freedom fighter, always said to him, "Algeria is in your hands now, my son."

How would he look himself in the mirror? Would he spit in his own face? He would never respect himself again. He was not prepared to pay such a high price, so he decided to continue on the battlefield until the end. Victory or death. He would often wake up in a panic, touching his neck. He wished to be killed by a bullet in the head or the heart, and that the killer's face not be the last thing he saw before departing this life. He swore he would not grant his killer this honor. As time passed, his body became accustomed to a strict schedule: He slept from 4 a.m. until 9 a.m., and if he did not respect this schedule, he would have a headache all day. Luckily, he found a helpful way to fight the insomnia. At night, he got into the habit of reading in the languages he knew. He would also watch films and listen to different types of music, including songs by Cheikh El Hasnaoui, Lounis Aït Menguellet, Lounès Matoub, Amar Ezzahi, Cheb Hasni, Jacques Brel, and Frank Sinatra. He still loved El Hasnaoui's song:

Oh night stars,
I stay up late with you.
I have neither beloved nor guardian
Anywhere in this country.

Soltani was not a fan of heartache, but sometimes memory is an open wound. Pressing on it with your finger makes it worse, and it takes longer to heal. Forgetting is better, or at least forgetfulness. It is not true that time heals all wounds. He still hasn't found a medicine or any other cure for a wounded memory.

When it was her turn to see the lawyer, the old woman stopped talking, got up, and wished Soltani well. He thanked her with a smile, then reached into his jacket pocket and pulled out his blue notebook. He looked through the notes he had taken earlier while reading through the copy of Falcon's file that Badrou Bouzar had given him.

What grabbed his attention was the newspaper interview with Falcon published in 1992, where he leveled dangerous accusations at Hoopoe. What had happened between them? Had their friendship soured that year? The file appeared to have been skillfully prepared. It might have been a genuine copy of the intelligence records, as it included telephone numbers along with a home and office address. Falcon's statements against Hoopoe were direct and blunt. The first conclusion he reached was that there was not just one Hoopoe. There was a huge difference between what he had heard from Badrou Bouzar and what he read in Falcon's statements. Was Hoopoe an angel or a devil?

After fifteen minutes, Soltani lifted his eyes from his blue notebook when he sensed someone standing in front of him. He easily recognized the lawyer from the picture published with the newspaper interview: thin, short, white-haired, wearing small-lensed glasses. He smiled and apologized for the long wait, politely showing the Colonel into his office. Soltani thanked him for seeing him without an appointment despite how busy he was.

"I'm like you, sir. Working on Independence Day."

"Algeria never really gained its independence. To this day, it remains colonized. The foreign colonizers left, and our brothers took their places, sir."

"You remind me of my father, may God have mercy on him. He used to say the same thing."

"Did your father fight during the Revolution?"

"He did. Then terrorists killed him in the '90s."

"May God have mercy on him and all the martyrs."

Soltani took a deep breath, then said: "They found Miloud Sabri slaughtered this morning."

Falcon was silent for a few seconds, then said, "'Verily we belong to God, and to Him we return.'"

"You knew him well, sir?"

"Only God knows him."

"He's your friend?"

"He was.... He was, sir."

"There were major disagreements between the two of you, correct?"

"Am I a suspect?"

"I just want to know the reasons for the disagreements."

Soltani took the notebook out from his jacket pocket and read some excerpts from the newspaper interview published in the summer of 1992: "'Miloud Sabri and his ilk are like parasites who will destroy Algeria.'... 'Miloud Sabri and his gang will drive the country into the abyss.'... 'He is among the most harmful people in this country.'... 'Miloud Sabri shares responsibility for wreaking havoc.'... 'Miloud Sabri did not serve Algeria for a single day. He always served his own interests.'"

Falcon listened to the quotes. He leaned back on his couch, saying: "Nothing but the truth, with the Lord as my witness."

"Why did you hate him so much, sir?"

"Have you heard of a person named Bernard Clavel?"

"No. Who's he?"

"He was one of the largest wine producers in western Algeria, and Hoopoe worked for him as a gardener. Clavel fled right before independence, and Miloud took ownership of his villa."

"What are you getting at?"

"We went from Clavel's colony to Hoopoe's colony, sir."

Falcon needed some air. He paused to alleviate the tension, walked to the window, and opened it. After taking a few breaths, he felt better. He walked back toward the Colonel and stressed that the difference between himself and people like Hoopoe was like the difference between the freedom fighter and the mercenary. The first one fought colonialism to free his country, then worked, and still worked, to build that country. The second one exploited the Revolution to get rich. These people never had Algeria's best interests in mind. Hoopoe and people like him destroyed the country and wanted to keep on destroying it. Falcon did not hide his feelings at all. He spoke with complete transparency, stating that the country would breathe a sigh of relief with his death, and hopefully, death would finish the job and reap the souls of his vile partners as well. "The knife has cut to the bone, and we cannot be silent about those mercenaries who replaced the honorable nationalists. Mercenaries are cancer cells that have spread throughout society. The only cure is to amputate the infected limbs at their roots without pity to save whatever can be saved.

"What a shame. Algeria, the country of martyrs, has become a country of cocaine, sir!"

Soltani was uneasy, so he turned toward the window to avoid Falcon's stern and sad gaze. The nasty business of cocaine. What a scandal. No one knew how it would end. Everything started when the navy seized 701 kilograms of pure cocaine from a steamer in the Port of Oran on May 29 that same year. It was valued at 30 million euros on the European market. The drugs were hidden in a shipment of meat from Brazil for a forty-year-old frozen meat importer. This importer had been transformed in no time at all from a butcher to a real estate contractor and one of the country's wealthiest people. He would give Umrah pilgrimage trips and luxury apartments as gifts to influential figures to facilitate his business interests.

Falcon said in a voice tinged with pessimism, "There's a lot of evidence implicating some important people in this scandal. Will investigators and judges have the courage to punish the perpetrators this time, or will it end with pinning the blame on scapegoats? Will the big fish be able to escape judgment's net as they have so many times before?"

Soltani returned to the topic at hand and detailed to Falcon how the body was discovered. He described the victim's bound hands and feet. He noticed that Falcon was somewhat troubled when he heard about the severed nose, as if it knocked him off balance. He sat back down, and Soltani exploited this to get information that might help him better understand his personality. Until now, he was the deceased's declared enemy, along with the political cartoonist Rachid Kadri.

"Do you know Miloud Sabri's nickname, sir?" Falcon asked.

"Yes. Hoopoe."

"And did you also know that the hoopoe is the only bird that defecates in its own nest?"

"Really?! Why would it do that?"

"To keep predators away from its young."

"How smart."

"But in doing so, it destroys the nest, sir."

"Tell me, what do you make of Hoopoe's severed nose, Mr. Talbi?"

"I'm against torture. Colonialism tortured me. And independence tortured me too."

Soltani noticed that Falcon neither boasted about nor made a show of crying about his arrest and torture or the death sentence handed down to him during the Revolution. Falcon added that he was just doing what needed to be done and that he was lucky to have remained alive while thousands of the best young people died. He seemed to regret his involvement in armed work.

"Would you like my frank opinion, Colonel?"

"Of course."

"Violence is contagious. Mahatma Gandhi was clever and knew what he was doing when he adopted the doctrine of nonviolence."

Soltani noticed that Falcon had a different perspective compared to other freedom fighters and the official history that justified everything and said that colonial violence was the sole cause of all other forms of violence, including Algerian fratricidal violence. According to the official view, all ills stemmed from a single source—colonialism.

"I have one last question, sir."

"Please, go ahead."

"You were part of a guerrilla group during the Revolution with the deceased, Miloud Sabri, also known as Hoopoe, and Zahra Misbah, I mean Dolores, right?"

"That's right."

"There was a fourth person named Abbas Badi, who went by 'Stork.' . . . He was the traitor . . ."

"Abbas didn't betray anyone . . . Abbas is a pure nationalist, beyond reproach!" said Falcon angrily.

"Okay, okay. Please, calm down. Where is he now?"

"God only knows."

"What's his story?"

"There's no use opening up old wounds, Colonel."

"But the past is the key."

He explained his theory to Falcon: The horrific way Hoopoe was murdered might be linked to a settling of old accounts that went back to the Revolution. Falcon did not find the theory very convincing and proceeded to enumerate the reasons why. First of all, it didn't make sense to take revenge on someone after sixty years. Secondly, Hoopoe was a man with business interests that were both domestic and foreign; no doubt, he had enemies who wanted to exact revenge on him for some harm he had caused them. Not to mention all the other damage he had caused that might have accounted for this unfortunate end.

"He who plants wind reaps storms."

"And the threatening postcards you all receive every year . . . ?"

"Who told you that? Dolores?"

"The source doesn't matter."

Falcon reached into a drawer and pulled out a box filled with cards with the same sentence written on them: "One of you is next." The Colonel noticed that some of them were old and some more recent. Falcon didn't attach any importance to these cards that came once a year, citing the French saying, "Those who say, don't do. And those who do, don't say." Whoever had an axe to grind and really wanted to take revenge wouldn't play the threat and intimidation game for more than half a century.

"All dogs bark, but only a few of them bite, Colonel."

Soltani thanked Falcon and left the office thinking about how similar Talbi and his own late father were. As he walked to where he had parked his car, he glanced at the old buildings that had fallen into disrepair and could not help but compare this poor neighborhood to the high-end neighborhoods with the luxury villas he had visited that morning. The Algeria of Falcon had no connection whatsoever to the Algeria of Miloud Sabri, Zahra Misbah, Youssef Misbah, and Badrou Bouzar. To each their own Algeria.

When he returned to the office, Soltani found the medical examiner, Abdou Hamlaoui, waiting for him. He had the preliminary results from his examination and autopsy report on Miloud Sabri. The Colonel realized that the Boss must have applied tremendous pressure—maybe even threatened him—for him to work so fast, especially on this particular day. Instead of spending the holiday with his family, playing with his kids, and enjoying the sun and the beautiful weather, here he was, tired and resentful. Would anyone thank him for his efforts?

The medical examiner placed his file on the desk and opened it. He took out a stack of pictures. A number of them were of the severed nose. Hamlaoui began by presenting three pictures of Hoopoe completely naked. His first conclusion was that the victim showed no signs of having been tortured, excluding the marks left on his hands and feet as a result of being tied to the bedposts. Then he focused on the severed nose where the cut marks appeared uneven. This meant that the victim had resisted. As for the slit throat, it was done in a straight line which meant that the victim was likely unconscious or already dead.

While Soltani was busy questioning the medical examiner about the body, Captain Samir Ziane appeared and gestured for him to step out onto the porch. The Colonel figured there was something important that could not wait. His aide informed him about secret ongoing investigations having to do with Hoopoe and others and their involvement in the cocaine scandal. The Colonel was sure this new information would turn the investigation upside down. The cocaine scandal was causing a significant uproar. As a result, the President of the Republic had relieved many generals of their duties, including the Secretary General for National Security, the Director of the Gendarmerie, senior officials in the Ministry of Defense, and other military leaders. Did Hoopoe's slaughter mark a qualitative shift in how disputes between conflicting government agencies were managed? Was General Belkacemi aware of this? And if so, why didn't he say anything?

8

Spring 1976

Miloud Sabri (aka Hoopoe), Zahra Misbah (aka Dolores), her sister Farida, Driss Talbi (aka Falcon), and their children all met for lunch every Sunday. Dolores saw to it herself that the table was correctly prepared. She wanted it filled with different types of fish—fried, grilled, sautéed, and steamed—presented with care and refinement. Her older daughter, Mona, ten years old, helped her put out the glasses and plates while Souad, two years younger, played with her cousin, Nabil.

Driss did not wait until they were done eating. He pulled a piece of paper out from his pocket and waved it around, smiling. Then he said in a loud voice, "There are still men in this country!"

He appeared to be directing his words at Hoopoe. He told him that he had obtained a copy of the statement against the Boumediene regime, signed by four well-known political figures: the first president of the interim government, Farhat Abbas; his successor, Benyoucef Benkhedda; the political activist, Hocine Lahouel; and Member of the National Assembly for the Revolution, Sheikh Mohamed Kheireddine. Falcon put on his glasses and proceeded to read the last part of the statement with fervor:

> Algerian men and women:
> The colonial regime that mobilized us against it humiliated us and prevented us from exercising national sovereignty in our own country by keeping us focused on problems related to food and the economy. Autocracy has gradually led us to the same place since our independence. We have neither freedom nor dignity. This submission is an insult to human nature in general and to Algeria in particular. It is also an insult to its character. For this reason, fighting men with good intentions have come together to denounce this situation and put a stop to the indignity that we face. They are appealing to Algerians to fight for the following:
>
> - First: Electing a sovereign constituent national assembly through a free democratic process
> - Second: Putting an end to the current authoritarian regime by placing legal barriers against every weak will of this kind
> - Third: Establishing freedom of expression and thought that the Algerian people have always fought for
> - Fourth: Striving for a united fraternal Arab Islamic Maghreb.

After he finished reading, Falcon folded up the piece of paper and put it back in his pocket. Then he removed his glasses and remarked, "The sacrifices of free patriots were not in vain."

Those who were there knew that he included himself. He had spent two years in prison from 1965 to 1967. After he got out, his wife, Farida, became pregnant and gave birth to a boy. They named him Nabil. Falcon returned to his studies, became a lawyer, and never backed down from his clear stance in criticizing the government. He used to say repeatedly that President Boumediene overthrew Ben Bella because of the latter's autocracy. But then, what did the new leader and his Revolutionary Leadership Council do but dissolve existing institutions, which included parliament, and seize all power? And why did Boumediene put Ben Bella in prison for more than ten years without trial? Hoopoe could not bear Falcon's commentaries, so he lit a Cuban cigar, following the fashion that Boumediene had started, which had become common among those in the know. He satisfied himself with a brief response.

"You know nothing at all about politics, brother."

"God bless you and those like you, Miloud."

Conversation between them was always sharp. Farida would avoid taking part, while Dolores would remain neutral. She was not entirely satisfied with Boumediene's politics, especially concerning his violations of human rights, which included torture. But at the same time, she confessed to liking him for uniting the country and keeping Algerians from killing one another and tearing the country apart. The six states that emerged during the Revolution would have become autonomous statelets after independence had it not been for Boumediene taking control of things.

"What do prominent members of the opposition want? In particular, those on the left, such as Mohammed Boudiaf and Hocine Aït Ahmed. Don't they want a socialist regime? How can one outdo the socialism of Boumediene, who established free education and healthcare and nationalized fossil fuels?" jeered a smiling Miloud.

Hoopoe became more influential as preparations were made for the referendum on the National Charter and the election of the only candidate, Houari Boumediene, as President of the Republic. There were rumors that he had been offered a seat in the new parliament but turned it down. Some people interpreted this stance by saying that he did not suffer from a thirst for power. Of course, he did not confirm or deny it, allowing the matter to remain cloaked in obfuscation, which only increased his power. In fact, he was laughing deep down inside at the confusion between power and government and the difference between the two. The first gives the orders, and the second carries them out.

During one of those evenings, surrounded by close friends, which included his brother-in-law, Youssef, Hoopoe said cheerfully, "Ah, Power, my magnificent lady! Who, or what, are you? Are you not a wonderful stage play with actors performing roles according to directions given by the director, who decides when they should move, when they should stand still, and even what expressions they should have on their faces? Then there's the audience, the people, who have no role whatsoever except to watch and clap. Isn't it better to remain behind the curtain and guide the actors?"

Falcon arrived during visiting hours. He went up to the second floor, where the cardiac disease unit was located. As he approached Stork's mother's room, he saw her standing in the doorway, speaking with a tall man dressed in Tuareg clothing. Then, before he left, she hugged and kissed him. Falcon ran after the man and started to yell: "Sir. Sir! SIR!"

The man turned around to look at him but didn't stop. Instead, he sped up and left through one of the side doors. Falcon ran after him but could not find him. It was as if he had vanished into thin air. After that, Falcon went to her room and asked her about the veiled man, but she denied he had even been there. Falcon did not persist. He did not want to annoy and wear her out. But why did she deny it? Was she hiding something? He could not stop thinking about the man. He began to rearrange his thoughts and tie together the various details. He remembered what Madame Febvre had said about the Tuareg clothes stolen from her house when he spoke with her in 1965. Suddenly, a thought occurred to him. Did Stork transform himself into a Tuareg after his nose was cut off? The veils Tuareg men wear would hide the severed nose!

The following day, Stork's mother died after a failed heart surgery. Falcon was certain that if Stork was alive, he would not miss the chance to view his mother's body one last time. He decided to act alone and in strict secrecy. He did not tell Hoopoe because he would not believe the story of the strange Tuareg and would only laugh at him. And this time, he would not hesitate to accuse him of being crazy. He realized that this was a golden opportunity to solve the mystery of Abbas Badi, aka Stork.

Throughout the wake, Falcon sat outside the casket room and waited. He drank multiple cups of coffee as they were offered to him. As time wore on, the visitors began to trickle out until there remained just a few women mourners around the casket. He stayed where he was and did not move. At dawn, he saw a person enter the house, so he pretended to be sleeping. After a few minutes, the man came closer, and there was the Tuareg. He entered the room to cast a final glance at the deceased. His visit lasted fifteen minutes, and when he left, Falcon got up and blocked his way as he said, "May God have mercy on your mother, Abbas."

"Amen."

Falcon was unable to hold back his tears. He walked up to Stork and hugged him. After a few seconds, the crying turned into broken sobs. The tears flowed and washed away years of pain, separation, longing, feelings of injustice, and lost dreams, big and small.

Stork paid his last respects to his mother from a distance. He did not want to take any chances and reveal his secret. After the burial rites were completed at Aïn Al-Baida Cemetery, Falcon invited his friend to the house he inherited from his grandmother in Mostaganem, and he agreed. They stayed there for two full days. Falcon avoided making his friend uncomfortable by asking him to remove the veil and listened to all the details, from the moment he fell into the clutches of Omar Mansouri to his flight from Oran dressed in Tuareg clothing. He was embraced by the desert south, where he found a place to settle down, with people who embraced him as family. After Dolores got married, thus destroying his dreams of love, Stork married Safia, the daughter of Mabrouk Agh Hassani. She was young, beautiful, and blind, so his disfigured face did not bother her. They were blessed with two children—Amina and Amal.

Falcon was not shy in scolding his friend for having disappeared all these years.

Stork explained that he had decided to contact only his mother because he was so worried about what the shock of the scandal and his sudden disappearance would do to her sick heart. He returned to Oran secretly to reassure her and gather information about his old comrades.

"Did you suspect me?" asked Falcon.

Stork replied after a moment's hesitation, "I did. The only ones who knew my whereabouts were you three."

"And now, do you trust me?" Falcon asked with a sad smile.

"Yes. After you were arrested in '65 and spent two years in prison, I was convinced you couldn't be the traitor. It was impossible."

"So, if you no longer suspect me, just two names remain."

"Hoopoe and Dolores."

"But this is impossible as well. How do you explain the threatening postcards Hoopoe, Dolores, and I have received every year since your disappearance back '62?"

"I don't know."

Before they parted ways, Stork took out a Qur'an and asked Falcon to swear on it not to tell a soul about this. Falcon tried to convince him that Hoopoe was a friend and that it was his right to know. He had been worried sick over him for years. But Stork was not convinced. Hoopoe might tell Dolores, and the old wounds would open up again. It was not in anyone's interest to dredge up the past. Falcon reluctantly swore not to divulge the secret. They agreed to meet again soon, this time down south, and of course, Stork insisted on reviewing all the details and arrangements. Falcon said jokingly, "As if you were still at war."

"My war goes on and on."

"But every war must end," added Falcon.

"Ever the optimist."

Stork walked to the window overlooking the sea and took in the view, remaining silent for a few minutes. He wanted to let go of his sorrows and cry out in anger and defeat, but he could not. Then he gathered up his courage, looked at his friend, and said in a sad voice, "Oh Lord. When will the nightmare I've been living for fourteen years end?!"

Driss could not think of anything to say, so he remained silent as Stork continued to lament his fate. He expressed his frustration at being unable to prove his innocence and restore his honor after his nose was cut like that of the worst traitors.

"I will not rest until I figure out who betrayed me and why. I fear I might die before uncovering the truth."

"May God help you."

Falcon met a veteran freedom fighter named Cherif Miqdad. He had come to seek his advice in a land dispute case with one of his relatives. Falcon discovered that the new client had been one of Omar's men. He started drawing him into conversation before asking him about Yazid's betrayal. Miqdad told him that he had been there when that young man's, Stork's, nose was cut off; he still remembered his name. Omar wanted just one thing, which was to avenge the killing of his cousin. And Omar had assured him that Stork was the one who did it.

"Omar was hasty and regretted it afterward."

"Why did he regret it?" asked Falcon.

"Poor Abbas was collateral damage."

"How so?"

"Yazid, may God have mercy on him, loved Algeria. He gave his life for it. He loved women too."

"What do you mean, Cherif?"

"Yazid was betrayed by his lover."

"Do you know who she was?"

"No, I don't."

"How about the one who ratted him out?"

"No."

Falcon tried to gather more details, but it was useless. Perhaps this man had not revealed the entire truth. Was he concealing the name of the lover and the identity of the snitch? And if so, why? Was he afraid of what would happen if he revealed them? It had been years since Stork's tragedy. Why be scared now? A thought occurred to him, which he tried to dismiss but could not. Was the traitorous lover Dolores? Falcon kept the story of Cherif Miqdad from Hoopoe and resolved to see what Stork said first.

The next day, he informed his wife, Farida, that he had to be in court in Algiers, but after flying to Algiers, he continued on to Tamanrasset. He arrived as the evening prayer was being called. Stork was stunned when he opened the door and saw his friend standing there before him. Baffled, he asked the reason for his visit. And had he stuck to the agreed-upon protocols?! Falcon reassured him that he had taken all the necessary precautions. He asked for some water to quench his extreme thirst. Then he told him the story of Cherif Miqdad from beginning to end.

"The bottom line is that Dolores is the one who betrayed Yazid."

"It is a distinct possibility."

"And whoever betrayed Yazid betrayed me."

"Correct."

They spent that entire night discussing it, going over the details again and again. They posed many questions and considered numerous theories. They remembered that Yazid had vehemently opposed the idea of Stork's and Dolores's marriage, so much so that words were exchanged. Not to mention the fact that he was the one who had recruited her. Was she really his lover? Dolores knew where Yazid's hideout was, as well as where Stork's hideout was, when Omar and his men grabbed him. Was she the traitor? If she was the one who betrayed him, what was the motive?

Falcon returned to Oran to confirm whether it was Dolores.

Necessary legal measures needed to be taken regarding the land dispute, and Cherif Miqdad visited Falcon's office many times, during which their relationship solidified. They were similar to one another in many respects. Neither one was happy about how the Revolution had turned out. Unlike other veterans, they did not chase after wealth and flatter the new rulers. A sense of trust began to take root between them. Falcon told his new friend of his concerns, then pressed him to tell the truth about Yazid's lover and reveal the identity of the one who betrayed Stork and caused this whole mess.

"Was Zahra Misbah, also known as Dolores, Si Yazid's mistress?" asked Falcon.

"No."

"You know her identity. Just tell me the truth, for God's sake!"

"Her nom de guerre was Suzanne."

"And her real name?"

"I don't know, but she's from Sidi Houari."

Falcon reached into his pocket and removed his wallet. He took out a black-and-white photo and showed it to Cherif, who glanced at it and then exclaimed in surprise, "That's Suzanne. She's the one who betrayed Yazid."

"Are you sure?"

"Very sure. Do you know her?"

"Yes, I know her well. She's my wife and the mother of my son."

"Oh my God!"

"She's the one who betrayed Abbas Badi too?"

"No, there was someone else."

"Who?"

"That's a secret."

"Why don't you just tell me the whole truth and put my mind at ease?"

"It's in your best interest and mine for it to remain a secret."

After Cherif Miqdad left his office, Driss called Hoopoe and shared all the details. He asked what to do about his wife, Farida. Hoopoe advised him not to act too quickly based on what might be no more than suspicions. He needed to gather solid evidence before accusing Farida of anything. He suggested they talk to Cherif Miqdad together to convince him to tell the entire truth and reveal all his cards. After going back and forth, they agreed to meet with him the following day.

When Falcon arrived home that evening, he found that neither Farida nor Nabil were there. Two minutes later, he heard a knock at the door. Their neighbor, Salwa, was standing there, holding Nabil by the hand. She explained that Farida had left the child with her for an hour but had not returned. Nabil was silent and refused to eat. Falcon thought he was just tired, so he took him to bed, where he closed his eyes and quickly fell asleep. He waited in vain for Farida to return. Then he called her sister, Dolores, and her brother, Youssef, as well as other acquaintances of hers, but no one could explain her sudden disappearance. At midnight, he went to the police station to file a report, after which he returned home very worried. He did not sleep that night. He sat close to the telephone, waiting for news, but it never came.

Early the next morning, he went to the kitchen to pour himself another cup of coffee to drive the sleep from his eyes. As soon as he sat down, he heard loud knocks on the door. He rushed to open it and found three police officers standing in front of him. The one in charge stepped forward and asked, "Are you the husband of Farida Misbah?"

"Yes," he said anxiously.

"It's about…"

"What happened to her?"

"May God reward you all. She drowned. It's likely she committed suicide," said the policeman.

Falcon heard footsteps behind him. He turned and saw his son, Nabil, standing there, tears streaming down his cheeks. Falcon embraced him.

Three days after Farida's funeral, Falcon, Dolores, and Hoopoe discussed Nabil's future. Falcon admitted that he could not care for a child who wasn't yet ten years old.

"The best solution is for Nabil to live with us," said Hoopoe.

"My nephew is also my son," said Dolores, holding back the tears.

"Exactly. There's no difference between him and my daughters Mona and Souad," added Hoopoe.

"I agree, but on the condition that he spend weekends with me."

That same day, Falcon received two phone calls. The first was from Stork, who expressed his condolences. Falcon took the opportunity to tell him that Dolores was innocent and that the true traitor had disappeared without a trace after independence. The second call was from Cherif Miqdad. He asked to see him as soon as possible. He sounded scared.

"They tried to kill me."

"Who?"

"I can't talk right now. I'll tell you everything when we meet."

"Where and when, Cherif?"

"Let's meet today at four, at the train station."

Falcon arrived fifteen minutes early. He waited a full hour, but there was no sign of him. He called Cherif's house, and his daughter answered, barely able to speak through her tears. She finally managed to say that her father had been killed in the elevator right after leaving the apartment to go to the midday prayer at the mosque. Falcon wondered whether the hand that killed Cherif Miqdad had something to do with his wife Farida's death as well.

Nabil remained silent for years. He wanted to share what he witnessed on the day his mother bid farewell to his father, but he chose to keep it to himself. He had seen and heard his mother crying as she spoke into the phone, and he still remembered what she said as she cried.

"God, I'm so tired. I'll confess to everything just to put my mind at ease."

After she hung up, he saw her get dressed to go out. Shaking, she leaned over and hugged him. She kissed him on his right cheek and then left. It was the last time she would kiss him.

9

Thursday, July 5, 2018

2:18 P.M.

Colonel Karim Soltani searched for a spot to park his car in November 1st Square. He walked up the stairs to the third floor of the building where the political cartoonist, Rachid Kadri, lived. Electric elevators in Oran were on their way to extinction; only a few of them still worked. Buildings had begun to deteriorate following the sale of state property to renters in 1981 and the phasing out of superintendents. He rang the bell for a sixth time. He guessed no one was inside and was about to turn around when he heard footsteps from behind the door. After a few seconds, a thick, bald man in his fifties with groggy, half-closed eyes opened the door. It seemed like he had just woken up from a deep sleep. He looked in his direction without really looking at his face and, sounding extremely annoyed, said, "What do you want?"

"I'm looking for Rachid Kadri."

"That's me."

"I'm Colonel Soltani from Anti-Terrorism. I'd like to speak with you."

"About what?"

"Do you want to talk about it here?"

Rachid Kadri stepped back from the entranceway to make room for him to pass, then closed the door. He indicated for Soltani to follow him. They walked into the small living room. Rachid took a Marlboro out of the pack and lit it. Then he handed a cigarette to the Colonel, who accepted it and thanked him. Soltani smoked Nassims, a local brand. He never switched to anything else despite the temptations of the more well-known international brands. It was not because of their price or out of zeal for the national product. It was just that old habits are hard to break. After they sat down, he looked at Rachid and, without introduction, asked him, "What's your relationship to Miloud Sabri?"

"No relationship at all."

"Should I remind you?"

Rachid shrugged his shoulders and said: "If you'd like."

"Souad."

"What do you want from me?" responded Rachid angrily.

"Answer my questions and I'll leave you alone."

The Colonel stepped over to the table and cast a glance at the caricature drawings scattered about. He admitted that he was a fan and that, like many readers, he loved Rachid's drawings, especially his recurring character, Brother Bandit. He asked him about the source of inspiration for this character, to which Rachid responded that art was mysterious, and that the artist relies on intuition. It might lead him to something that hadn't occurred to him before. Art is a tangle of coincidences—an adventure in the fullest meaning of the word. You might know where you're starting from, but who knows where it will lead? Soltani stopped him there before he could continue theorizing and avoid talking about Brother Bandit.

"Do you know what word Hoopoe used a lot?" the Colonel asked, flipping through the scattered drawings.

"I don't know. What is it, sir?"

"'Brother.'"

"For real? What a coincidence! I told you."

The Colonel continued to rifle through the drawings. He stopped at a picture that looked like Brother Bandit, but without a nose, and began to examine it. He thought it likely that this drawing was new because the paper was clean compared to the others. Had he drawn it yesterday or today? Or to be more specific, before Hoopoe was killed, or after?

He decided to play his winning card. He might get some useful information that would move the investigation forward. Time was passing quickly, and he needed some concrete results. Soltani walked toward Rachid and looked at him seriously as he announced, "Hoopoe died this morning."

"God curse him."

"Only mercy is allowed for the dead, Mr. Kadri."

"I'm free to say what I want."

"Would you like to know how he died?"

"It doesn't matter."

"He was slaughtered like an Eid sheep."

Soltani went back to the table. He picked up the drawing of Brother Bandit with the severed nose and waved it in front of Rachid.

"We found Hoopoe's body this morning, his nose cut off, and here you've drawn Brother Bandit without a nose. Please don't tell me this was a result of 'artist's intuition.'"

"Life is full of coincidences, sir."

Soltani thought about how much Rachid used the word "coincidence." Was it to tease and provoke him? He wasn't convinced. He thought that following the thread of the noseless Brother Bandit would lead somewhere. The severed nose had been placed on Hoopoe's chest like a medal. The intention to send a message was clear.

"Where were you last night and at dawn this morning, Mr. Kadri?"

"Here at home, working."

"You stayed here? You didn't go out?"

"Correct."

"Were you alone?"

"Yes."

"Is there anyone who can attest to that?"

"No."

"He who has no witnesses is a liar, Mr. Kadri."

Truth be told, Soltani didn't attach much importance to witnesses. Criminals will often arrange for fake alibis. Rachid got up from his chair and looked at his guest.

"Would you like a glass of tea? All I have is tea and water."

"No, thank you."

Rachid went to the kitchen. Soltani took the opportunity to take some pictures with his phone of photos hanging on the wall. He told himself he would take a closer look at them later. The photos were somewhat old. Rachid looked like a fresh-faced youth, always smiling. He looked happy and cheerful—nothing like the Rachid of today. His youthfulness was gone, and old age had crept into his face and body.

Five minutes later, Rachid returned to the living room carrying a glass of tea for himself. Then he lit another cigarette without bothering to offer one to his guest this time. He sat without saying a word and looked up at the ceiling as if stuck in a difficult situation. It seemed as if his mood had suddenly changed.

Soltani stood up and ordered Rachid not to leave Oran, as he might need him to answer more questions. Rachid replied that he hadn't left Oran in years and that living anywhere else would make him feel like a fish out of water. The sense of freedom he felt here made it impossible for him to go anywhere else. Rachid's mood suddenly shifted yet again, and he proceeded to tell the story of himself and Oran. He had come here from his birthplace, Mascara, to study fine arts and never left. Soltani decided to just listen as he talked. He might leak something useful that could help with the investigation, even a single word that could turn things on their head. Who knows? He might forget himself and reveal some secrets. Sometimes people confess to a crime without even knowing it.

Suddenly, Rachid stopped talking when he heard a noise. Someone was turning a key in the lock. The Colonel looked at Rachid and noticed his discomfort. His face turned into a frown, and his hands seemed to shake slightly.

A few moments later, a tall, svelte young woman with long hair and kohl darkening her wide eyes came in. She was wearing a long brown dress and black sandals. She greeted them with a smile. Soltani expected Rachid to introduce her, but he didn't. He remained utterly silent, so the Colonel spoke to her directly.

"I'm Colonel Soltani from Anti-Terrorism."

"Hello. I'm Zuhour."

"Zuhour, a friend's daughter, has come to visit me," said Rachid, breaking his silence, a bit agitated.

"Your friend's daughter has a key to your apartment?" the Colonel quipped.

"That's right, Colonel," answered Rachid.

"How old are you?" the Colonel asked the young woman.

"Twenty."

"Your ID card, please."

Zuhour looked through her wallet and handed him the card. The Colonel confirmed that she was not a minor. She had told him the truth about her age. But something important grabbed his attention.

"Last name, Badi. Any relation to Abbas Badi?"

"No."

He handed the card back and looked her in the eyes. He had an uncanny ability to read what people don't say out loud. People don't only speak with their tongues. The movements of their hands, how they look, their lips, and their eyelashes all say what the tongue does not wish to reveal. The Colonel turned to go and again asked Rachid not to leave Oran without permission.

When he reached the ground floor of the building, he called his aide, First Lieutenant Derraji, and asked her to look into Zuhour Badi, born on August 14, 1998, in Tamanrasset. He added that the young woman denied any connection to Abbas Badi, aka Stork.

He set off to rest for a little bit at the Theatre Café, where the great playwright Abdelkader Alloula used to go, before his assassination during Ramadan in 1994. Sitting and sipping his coffee there, he felt like he was offering a prayer over Alloula's pure soul. As soon as he sat down, his eyes fell on a large poster for *The Battle of Algiers* by Gillo Pontecorvo. This film fed the imaginations of generations of Algerians. It was shown more than once a year on public television stations on national holidays such as November 1 (the start of the Revolution) and July 5 (Independence Day). Like the rest of his peers, when the Colonel was a child, he was dazzled by the character Little Omar, who met his fate with Ali La Pointe and Hassiba Ben Bouali. He was even sometimes jealous of him. If only he had lived during the Revolution and fought alongside the guerrilla warriors. He would have thrown the colonists out too.

He started to view this film differently in the '90s when terrorism worsened, and Algerians started blowing up other Algerians. Exploding packages were planted in public places crowded with people, like markets and stations. One time, he interrogated a terrorist after a car bomb was detonated in a public market. The man confessed to more than one operation. He still remembered the conversation that took place between them.

"I'm a mujahid fighter and a guerrilla warrior."

"You're a terrorist criminal and a son of a bitch!" shouted the Colonel.

"I'm like Ahmed Zabana, Saâdi Yacef, and Ali La Pointe. Didn't the colonial authorities call them terrorists too?"

"They brought about independence for the country. You all just destroy things and turn them to shit!"

"We're fighting in the path of God. And we will complete the path with God's permission. God is with us."

God is with us! Soltani asked himself so many times about the source of this blind faith. How had they arrived at this state of contentment? He recalled his years at the University of Bouzareah in Algiers in the late '80s and early '90s. He was a student in the Department of English at the Language Institute. He remembered discussions he had with Islamists who chanted the slogan: "'No charter or constitution,' said God and the Prophet." He would debate them, saying that the Qur'an required interpretation. Why look at things so simplistically? One time, one of them tried to convince him that Islam was the solution to all problems, without exception. Soltani asked about how Islam would deal with unemployment. The Islamist responded confidently that the solution lay in requiring women to stay at home and only employing men. That way, they could solve two problems at once: unemployment *and* the temptation that comes from mixing between the two sexes.

He stopped the turning wheel of memory when the waiter put his cup of coffee down on the table and rushed off to attend to the other customers' orders. The memories flowed back after the first two sips. One event left a deep impression on him, opening his eyes to how dangerous things were. During the 1990–91 academic year, Islamists at the University of Algiers planned to divide the cafeteria into two: the ground floor for men and the upper floor for women. At the time, he and others rejected this division, and discussion raged between those who supported it and those who opposed it. One of the veiled students complained that she couldn't eat with men staring at her, especially as she put a spoon into her mouth. She was too embarrassed to finish what she was saying, but those sitting there understood that she meant something sexual. Where did this creature want to live? In a society composed solely of women?! In any case, the discussion produced nothing memorable. Instead, it developed into a full-scale verbal brawl. The following day, he arrived at the cafeteria at lunchtime and found bearded men at the entrance. They were not students and were brandishing weapons, threatening everyone who went in. Who had allowed them onto campus? Were the security officials working with them? Who had given them this false sense of strength, that they could do whatever they wanted? After a few days, he ran into that female student who was so ardent about separating men from women in the university cafeteria at the university bus station. It was indescribably crowded, bodies pushed up against one another, a confused tangle. He gave her a sympathetic look as he watched her wrestle with her colleagues to get up onto the bus. That day, he realized that the problem with the Islamists was that they were more concerned with nonsense than they were with dealing with real problems.

He did not continue his university career, stopping before completing his master's. In 1993, terrorists slaughtered his father in Blida because he had refused to allow them to use his house. Soltani left the university and joined the army to do his military service in Oran. After two years, he joined the Anti-Terrorism Unit, and due to his mastery of languages, he was assigned to a unit operating under the cover of a translation office in Oran. He made his way up through the ranks until he became a colonel and was now head of this unit, which included Captain Samir Ziane and First Lieutenant Malika Derraji, both of whom he had chosen himself because they had mastered several foreign languages.

He finished his coffee, drank a glass of water, and left the Theatre Café. He headed to where he had parked his car.

Soltani returned to the office by way of Rue Larbi ben M'hidi. When he got to the Murdjajo Cinema, he called his lover, Meriem, but she didn't answer. She was still angry. He felt his headache worsen, so he popped two aspirins into his mouth and chased them with a gulp of water. Two minutes later, he received a call from General

Belkacemi. He asked how things were going with the investigation, so the Colonel told him about his meetings with Badrou Bouzar, Driss Talbi, and Rachid Kadri. He didn't mention Hoopoe's possible involvement in the cocaine case. That needed some more investigation.

Soltani found the criminal report on his desk. The part about the prints found on the dagger drew his attention. They were a perfect match with Badrou Bouzar. He called the clinic immediately and was told he had left without the doctors' permission. Was Badrou the killer? The scenario was completely unclear. There were too many holes. If he were truly the killer, then why did he call in the crime in the first place? Why did he leave the dagger—the murder weapon—under the pillow? He must have forgotten it there because it didn't make sense that he left it there on purpose. He already knew the prints would lead directly to him. The Colonel remembered the scene of Badrou fainting when he saw the dagger that morning. Perhaps he had seen it, or even used it, before.

Little by little, a new theory began to form in his mind: Perhaps someone was looking to frame Badrou Bouzar for the murder of Hoopoe. Badrou was not stupid; he might have realized that someone wanted to lure him to the villa and implicate him. Someone sent the text message early in the morning from Hoopoe's phone. This was a reasonable theory. But if Badrou really was innocent, why would he run rather than face the investigation head-on?

10

Winter and Spring 1986

That morning in early January, the university was unusually lively, teeming with journalists, National Liberation Front officials, and local authorities, accompanied by their drivers and bodyguards—a crowd of men in dark suits and ties standing out against the backdrop of students in jeans or robes recently imported from the Gulf. They had come to hold a rally for the January 16 referendum, which was meant to ratify the new National Charter, a revised version of the state's ideological manifesto. Shortly before the event began, the young Badrou Bouzar—who was in his third year of law school and, more importantly, one of the leaders of the Islamist student movement—was approached by the officer in charge of university security.

"Stay out of trouble."

"He who is silent to the truth is nothing more than a mute devil."

"Take your anger out on the communists and stay away from the Liberation Front."

"There's no difference between the Liberation Front and the heretical communists."

"Listen to what I'm saying, my boy."

"The words of God and the Prophet take precedence."

"You'll regret it."

Badrou Bouzar did not take this threat seriously. He planned on confrontation without regard to the consequences. "We need to sacrifice for this religion," he said enthusiastically to his brothers in the university mosque.

The large auditorium was packed, with the most prominent members of the party seated on the stage or in the front row, while Miloud Sabri, aka Hoopoe, sat in the second row, blending in with the audience, listening and taking notes. Badrou chose a spot in the middle of the room so he could see everyone, and so security would not be able to silence and easily remove him. He listened to what the party representatives had to say before the opportunity to speak was given to the students. He was extremely irritated when the student communist leader accused the Liberation Front Party of surrendering to reactionary forces and cited the Family Law, ratified in 1984, as an example. The leader said it was insulting to women and imported from backward religious systems.

Badrou Bouzar put his hand up to speak and was handed the microphone. He stood up where he was, smoothed out his long white *qamees*, and began in the name of God with the *basmala* and praise for the Prophet, may peace and blessings be upon him. Then he confirmed that he opposed the current constitution completely and absolutely because the only acceptable constitution was what God said in the Qur'an and what has been transmitted from the Prophet Muhammad—peace and blessings be upon him—in the blessed Sunna. He stopped for a moment and looked at those seated around him. Then he raised his voice.

"The only solution is to implement Islamic Sharia law!"

He proceeded to enumerate the evils of socialism and its harsh consequences. He concluded by saying, "The Liberation Front is a communist party."

Raucous applause filled the room, and one of the representatives of the "single party" who had spoken before set out to convince him that communism and socialism were different and that Islam does not oppose socialism, citing the positions of Abu Dharr al-Ghifari, one of the companions of the Prophet. But Badrou Bouzar did not lend his words any credence. The discussion turned into a debate between him and the student communist leader, each one speaking his mind. The two opposing sides presented many different points of view and proposed various solutions. However, one point on which they agreed was placing responsibility for the country's economic, social, political, cultural, and moral crises on the Liberation Front Party.

Hoopoe followed the discussion between the communist and the Islamist student with interest and delight. He thought it was rare to find young men from the Liberation Front Party as well-armed with arguments, boldness, and enthusiasm. They had started talking like sheikhs, fed like sheep on the same loose slogans. Hoopoe had made it a habit of using metaphors from the world of horses that he loved so much. He saw the Islamist student as a purebred horse. Ah, if only he could lead him by the reins. No good could be hoped for from the communist student. Had he appeared in the '60s or '70s during the height of the agricultural revolution or the great nationalizations, there might have been a role for him. As for now, the winds were blowing in favor of the Islamists. The future was theirs.

When the discussion was over, the security official stormed up to Badrou and said to him in a voice that everyone could hear, "You've crossed the line. The one who disobeys gets the rod, you dog!"

"I fear no one but God."

Things almost boiled over, but Hoopoe intervened with carefully chosen words.

"We all want what's best for Algeria."

His words were well received, especially by the security official, who was quick to say, "When Miloud Sabri, the famous Hoopoe, the great freedom fighter, speaks, we need to listen...and obey." He accompanied this praise with an embrace and a kiss.

"All of us are working in the country's best interests to solve the problems it faces," said Hoopoe, aiming his words at Badrou as he stepped aside.

"Socialism is the problem, and the Islamic State is the solution," responded Badrou in a voice that betrayed no doubt.

"Things are complicated," added Hoopoe.

"I have left you two things, and as long as you hold on to them, you will not go astray: God's book and His Prophet's Sunna. Believe the Prophet, and peace and blessings be upon him," Badrou Bouzar said enthusiastically.

"You're very passionate, my boy. You remind me of when I was young during the Revolution."

Hoopoe asked the student his name and what he was studying. Then they exchanged some words about Islam's role in society's development and education. They paused on the perplexing question as to why Muslims had fallen behind while others advanced. Hoopoe asked Badrou to visit him in his office to continue the conversation. He gave him his card.

Three days later, the university security official followed through on his threats and ordered Badrou to leave the university premises immediately, citing legal reasons. He didn't have the right to stay in university housing because, technically, he resided in Oran. He tried appealing to the administration, but it was no use. It became clear to him that the punitive measures against him would not stop there. They might even expel him from the university. Badrou needed to find a solution before it was too late. After much thought, it occurred to him to call Hoopoe. He was surprised the man still remembered his name and was happy to meet with him two hours later.

Badrou headed to Hoopoe's office on Rue Loubet downtown and was greeted warmly. Hoopoe had him sit on a fancy couch and treated him like an important guest. He gave Badrou a choice between coffee and tea. He chose tea. They exchanged some comments about the university symposium, then Badrou broached the subject of the harassment he was being subjected to. Hoopoe listened intently, then reached behind him for the phone and made a call that lasted no more than two minutes. Rarely did Badrou see a person like him who applied the well-known rule that the best way to speak is to keep it short and to the point. He ended the call by thanking the person on the other end and repeating a sentence that would ring in Badrou's ears afterward: "If you need anything, I'm here, brother."

Smiling, he hung up the phone and said, "Your problem is a thing of the past."

"Thanks so much, Mr. Miloud."

"Call me Uncle Miloud."

"May God make more people like you, Uncle Miloud."

That meeting lasted two and a half hours, all spent discussing politics and religion. Badrou talked more than Hoopoe as he showered him with questions. He was very curious. Badrou told him of his dream to achieve martyrdom in God's path. Then he talked about his plan to join the mujahideen in Afghanistan, as had hundreds of other young Algerian men. These men went to the holy places to perform the Umrah and found everything they needed there, provided by the Saudis, to go to Karachi in Pakistan. And from there to Afghanistan to undertake jihad. Miloud expressed how pleased he was with Badrou and his readiness to sacrifice for his principles.

Hoopoe was familiar with the ins and outs of the Afghan issue. He considered the ongoing war a proxy war. He lit his Cuban cigar and explained his theory: People fight to gain the upper hand that will allow them to negotiate from a stronger starting point. The United States is the one driving what is referred to as "jihad" in Afghanistan, with the help of Pakistan and Saudi Arabia. The motive is not religious or political but, rather, economic. The capitalist system always needs new markets.

"The world is changing, my boy, and we need to get used to it before it's too late."

"The only solution is Islam, Uncle Miloud."

"Yes...but political Islam, my son!"

"Islam cannot be broken apart. It comprises politics, culture, education, economics, and science."

"But politics is what governs everything," laughed Hoopoe.

Hoopoe conceded that socialism had failed in Algeria, from Ahmed Ben Bella to Chadli Bendjedid to Houari Boumediene. Badrou asked him about the reforms President Bendjedid had called for, to which Hoopoe responded that reform was like an exterior restoration. The problem was with the foundation. Algeria was like a shaky, damaged house after an earthquake. Would restoration be enough? He concluded his analysis, saying, "The house needs to be torn down and rebuilt."

"How, Uncle Miloud?"

"That's the shepherd's job."

"And the flock?"

"To stay silent and follow orders."

Badrou didn't fully absorb what Hoopoe said because he was hearing it for the first time, but he was very much drawn in by it.

Badrou Bouzar returned to the university residences and found the security official waiting for him. He gave him a king's welcome. The official apologized for mistreating him and promised a fresh start. Badrou was shown a single room as a sign of the official's good intentions, but he turned it down. He feared for his reputation at the university and the suspicions that would inevitably surround him. What Badrou learned from this incident was that Miloud Sabri held a great deal of power and that he might be able to help him in the future. He had hated life ever since he was born in the poorest neighborhood in Oran, Sidi El Bachir. The kids who grew up there had but two choices—going astray or following the path of religion. Most of his childhood friends went astray and took up stealing, then went to prison, as was the case with his friend Redouane Derbal. Badrou was lucky not to follow that path. He found his way in the mosque, praying constantly and attending religious lessons that volunteers gave in various subjects. His grades improved and he passed the middle school exams, after which he went on to high school, then to university. The mosque was his true home. Sometimes, he would sleep there to study religion and memorize the Qur'an. Badrou was addicted to listening to taped sermons of the greatest preachers, such as Abd al-Hamid Kishk. He also read Islamic magazines and books assiduously. He loved Sheikh Abdullah Yusuf Azzam and his famous book, *The Signs of the Merciful in the Jihad of the Afghans*. He was very much affected by it. With his brothers, he would recount the miracles it described, such as when a Soviet tank ran over an Afghan mujahid and he lived. Or the story of another mujahid who, after reciting some Qur'anic verses and supplications, threw a handful of dirt at a tank, and it exploded just like that. He was able to help his friend, Redouane Derbal, get away from the world of crime. Redouane repented under his guidance and came to follow him like a shadow. Redouane's mother was thrilled that her son had returned to the right path, and she would wish Badrou the best whenever she saw him.

Zahra, aka Dolores, was surprised to see the young, bearded man in a long white robe sitting in Hoopoe's office for a second time.

"What does he want with my husband? More to the point, what does Miloud want with him?" she mumbled to herself, smiling.

The success of the Iranian Revolution seven years prior and Imam Khomeini's rising star made Hoopoe recalculate and reconsider his bets. He became convinced that the future belonged to the Islamists. They had succeeded in Iran. They had assassinated Anwar Sadat in Egypt. And perhaps they were on their way to defeating the Soviets in Afghanistan. Dolores couldn't stand the Islamists because they used religion to achieve their political goals. Their strength increased after Houari Boumediene's death. The new president, Chadli Bendjedid, gave in and made many concessions to them, the most important of which was the Family Law that the parliament of the "single party" had ratified two years prior. It made women minors for life. That same day, Dolores commented in a voice tainted with anger and heartbreak, "Now I need my guardian's—meaning my husband, father, or brother's—permission to live my own life?

Amazing! I didn't have to ask for permission when I joined the fight for independence!"

Driss Talbi, aka Falcon, followed what was happening in the country with trepidation. Basic foods such as sugar, oil, semolina, coffee, eggs, and potatoes were all but gone from the market. He asked a neighbor, an official in one of the markets, why staples were so scarce. He told him in a lowered voice so no one would hear that food was actually there in abundance, that tons of sugar, oil, semolina, and dried goods were piled up in storehouses because orders had been issued from above not to distribute them.

"Sons of bitches! They've put the people in a cage, and now they're starving them!" Falcon fumed.

Falcon was convinced the country was being driven off a cliff. His daily interactions with people on the street and in the courts made him fear the coming explosion. With the drop in oil prices, things began to worsen at the start of 1985. Of course, that was the official explanation. What was really going on was a rise in corruption and embezzlement of public funds. Despite the machine of oppression and persecution that existed, some signs of opposition were beginning to show among the people. During one of his secret visits to Stork in Tamanrasset, Falcon criticized President Chadli Bendjedid's policies. Instead of beneficial reforms to the socialist experiment, he reversed the most important gains the people had made over the last decade, such as free medical care and education for all. He wondered what would happen to free citizens like himself who had opposed his predecessor, President Boumediene. Would they end up actually pining for him?

"Will you admit that you were wrong about Boumediene?" Stork playfully chided him.

"I'm terrified of that."

Meanwhile, Falcon was determined to try his luck again with marriage. Ten years had passed since his wife Farida's mysterious death, and Nabil had become a young man. Falcon met a middle school teacher, and they got married. Months after the wedding, she had not become pregnant, so he went to a medical specialist friend in search of an explanation. After the examination and necessary tests, he asked Falcon to come and talk with him alone, insisting that his wife not come. Falcon was surprised by the request. But he understood why as he listened to the bitter truth.

"You can't have children because your testicles are damaged," said the doctor sadly.

Falcon went to other doctors for a second opinion, but the initial diagnosis stood. He had been subject to torture on two separate occasions, first in 1958 under the French and then in 1965 following independence. The torturers preferred the sensitive areas of the body.

Falcon tried to avoid the nasty question that hovered around his head like a stubborn, dirty fly, but was unsuccessful. If he could not have children, then Nabil was not his son. Who was the biological father, then? Who did his first wife, Farida, betray him with? Should he tell his comrades, Stork, Hoopoe, and Dolores, the truth? Should he come clean to Nabil and destroy his life forever?

He decided to keep the secret from everyone.

11

Thursday, July 5, 2018

3:34 P.M.

Colonel Karim Soltani called his aide, Captain Samir Ziane, and asked him to focus on Badrou Bouzar, look into his origins and background. Did he have an active role investing in terrorism in Libya? Was he, like Hoopoe, involved in the cocaine case? As soon as he hung up, First Lieutenant Malika Derraji knocked on the door. She was holding a red notebook where she jotted down thoughts, tables, sketches, and notes as they occurred to her. She sat down and told Soltani, "We have a major love story here, sir."

"Who's our Juliet?"

"Juliet is Souad Sabri, Hoopoe's daughter."

"And Romeo?"

"Rachid Kadri."

Derraji was adept at storytelling, particularly when it came to love stories. Having listened to, read, and watched many, she knew exactly how to start and finish a tale.

With great precision, she chose where to introduce dramatic pauses, keeping the suspense high. She paid close attention to the main characters without neglecting the secondary ones, understanding that even the most minute details were crucial to comprehending complex stories.

The First Lieutenant focused on the essential elements that no love story worthy of the name would lack. For example, the two lovers, Souad and Rachid, faced significant obstacles that threatened to separate them, but they remained steadfast until the end. They were prepared to pay any price for their love, no matter how high. There are many classical ingredients to a successful love story. For example, the woman belongs to a wealthy, well-known family and the man belongs to a poor, unknown family. And in the end, the woman dies by her lover's hand. Real love stories have tragic endings, from Romeo and Juliet to the Algerian tale of Hiziya and her cousin Saïd. Death is the ultimate obstacle, the most dangerous enemy of lovers. The general rule in these stories is that one lover's death leaves behind a lost love that is remembered for generations to come.

Derraji pointed to Rachid Kadri's psychological state after Souad's murder. His journey began in the dark corridors of depression as he swung from one extreme to the other: stability to turmoil, excitement to sadness, zeal to frustration, optimism to pessimism. In sum, his mental state was volatile.

"Meaning he could kill in a moment of weakness."

"It's a possibility, sir."

As she glanced at her notebook, Derraji added that Rachid Kadri was among those closest to Driss Talbi, aka

Falcon. It might have been a mutual hatred for Hoopoe that brought them together. Their friendship dated back to the uprising of October 1988, when Rachid was arrested and tortured, and later testified in the human rights forum that Falcon had established. Rachid and Souad were in the same apartment when they were fired upon; he was wounded, whereas she was killed immediately.

When Derraji got up to leave, Soltani asked her whether she had found any information on Zuhour Badi. She replied that she had contacted some people and was waiting for their response. She would let him know of anything new as soon as she heard back.

Soltani called Meriem again, but she still didn't answer. There was no way to appease her other than to keep calling until she was ready to pick up. Meriem was not just another one of his sexual conquests. He had realized from the start that this one would not be fleeting. He met her three years ago. He was visiting a friend, a police inspector, at a police station close to the Zabana Museum when he saw her for the first time. What caught his attention was her long hair, which looked like a horse's tail. He was also taken by the way she dressed. She wore jeans, a white high-collared shirt, a brown leather jacket, and black shoes with a medium heel. Meriem was furious; she was screaming. It was not easy to calm her down, but finally, she regained her composure. She said she was a gynecologist at the University of Oran Hospital. She had come in with a twenty-year-old woman. Two young men from her neighborhood had repeatedly harassed the woman, and she wanted to file a criminal complaint for fear of being raped. The wait was longer than it needed to be, and Meriem just lost it. Soltani stepped in to complete the paperwork.

After submitting a copy of the complaint, the young woman left. Soltani took the opportunity to invite Meriem for a cup of coffee, and she accepted. They looked for a nearby cafeteria but had a hard time finding one. Even though Oran was a city largely unfettered by tradition, the vast majority of cafés were still monopolized by men. As soon as they sat down, they started to banter. He boasted of his roots in the capital city of Algiers, and she boasted of hers in Tlemcen and al-Andalus, medieval Muslim Spain.

"Had I been born now, I would have been named Maria instead of Meriem."

"It's very much in vogue here. In Europe, though, it seems old-fashioned."

"I've heard people say that naming girls Maria is part of the traditional Sunna."

"For real? How so?"

"It has to do with Maria the Copt, one of the Prophet's wives," replied Meriem.

They talked for more than an hour about all sorts of things and discussed numerous questions: Could they believe that guys were harassing the girls in the neighborhood? Where had the chivalry of the old days gone? They talked about how light and heavy drug use had skyrocketed among adolescents and how violence of all types (psychological, verbal, and physical) had spread like wildfire. They discussed what role parents should play in raising their children. What was the value of religion when it failed to uplift society's noble traits? Was there any hope for the future? May God help us. What had happened to the Algerians? Had the years of terrorism in the '90s burned everything to the ground? Their chitchat wasn't limited to just these types of questions and observations about the fate of the country and its people, either. But Soltani was preoccupied with other things. For example, whether or not she was married. He hoped deep down that she was not. He did not invest feelings in married women because the benefits were few, and the risks were significant. Besides, there were enough women for everyone. He discovered some details of the beautiful doctor's life without having to resort to his experience in investigation and interrogation. Meriem was an open book. She told him in no uncertain terms and without shyness that she was divorced. Then, she explained the situation to him frankly and directly.

"In our country, divorced women are considered sexual time bombs that might go off at any moment."

"Careful what you say. Time bombs are at the heart of my work in anti-terrorism."

She looked at him and could not resist the urge to laugh. He laughed as well. At the end of that meeting, they exchanged phone numbers.

The following day, he called her, and they agreed to meet for lunch. As they got to know one another better, he started to call her by a pet name, "Meryouma," rather than Meriem. He tried to kiss her two weeks after they met, but she turned her face away. Then she gave him a bitter smile and whispered in his ear, "Too bad, you're just like the others."

She left angry, and he regretted his actions, which he beat himself up over. He called her numerous times, but she did not answer. So, he went to the university hospital, braving the awful smell of the wards, and asked for her. He found her, apologized, and proceeded to repeat a snippet of an Amar Ezzahi song:

Oh, Meryouma, may God guide you, may God guide you.
Which heart loves you, loves you?
My Lord created you as best as can be.
From you, my soul is bereft, oh Meryouma.
To spend my life in your hands, I'm forever doomed, oh Meryouma.

She laughed and said, "You're crazy, I swear. Crazy."

They started seeing each other again. He had learned a good lesson and swore only to shake hands rather than try to kiss her again. They met twice a week. Their eyes revealed what words could not, and they did not feel that the fifteen-year age difference would get in their way.

Three months later, she invited him to her thirty-second birthday party at her house, and he accepted. It was a chance to meet her two sisters and her closest friends. At the end of the evening, she asked him to stay, telling him she wanted him for something. After everyone left, he sat in the living room sipping a glass of Algerian Saint-Augustin wine and listening to a song ("In Love, There's Always a Loser") sung in French by Julio Iglesias. He heard footsteps behind him, so he turned around and found Meriem standing there wearing a short blue nightgown. His heart skipped a beat. She came close and kissed him passionately as if drinking to quench the thirst of a sweltering day. Then she took his hand and led him to her bed. She moved toward him with unbridled passion. No woman had ever desired him as Meriem did that night.

He wanted to take full advantage of a few moments of privacy in the office to think through the investigation, but it did not last long. Captain Ziane came with his papers and brought his iPad this time too. He was grinning like a fisherman returning to shore with a full net. He sat down and said, "Badrou Bouzar has been an informant since 1988."

"What's his area of expertise?"

"Spying on Islamists and hunting terrorists, sir."

Soltani was not surprised that Badrou had been enlisted as an informant. It was no secret that the Islamists had been infiltrated since the beginning. The question was, what did he get in return? Money? Power? Protection? Badrou Bouzar's name did not appear anywhere in the political arena. Had he followed Hoopoe's strategy of hiding backstage and directing the actors from there? Perhaps he understood that money and politics did not need to appear together in broad daylight but instead could exist as secret lovers. Acting out in the open is extremely dangerous and can provide enemies with the opportunity for revenge. Captain Ziane confirmed that

Badrou was a model Islamist according to how Islamism manifested in Algeria: He had held on to his original name, Badreddine, which had a religious ring to it. Then, he started to loosen up and encouraged people to call him by his nickname, Badrou. Like his name, his beard went through numerous stages as the years passed. At first, it was long and thick, covering his entire face. Then he started to limit its scope until it was shorter and came to just encircle his lips.

"There are lots of business arrangements between Hoopoe and Badrou," Ziane said.

"Including through marriage?"

"That's one of them, sir."

In 1997, the husband of Hoopoe's older daughter, Mona, died of lung cancer due to smoking. However, it seemed that cancer was only the final torment suffered by the poor man. Mona could not have children. They tried all sorts of ways to get pregnant, but none of them worked. As a result, her husband's life became a living hell. She blamed him and poured her anger out on him by insulting him publicly and forcing him to take care of her dogs. Badrou knew about this ahead of time, but he proposed to her anyway and suffered the consequences, which included remaining childless. This marriage could only be described as an "arrangement." Did Badrou regret it afterward? Did he receive compensation for the troubles he endured? Why didn't he take a second wife, even secretly? Was he afraid of Hoopoe's wrath?

"This marriage opened the gates of heaven for Badrou."

"And the gates of hell, sir."

Ziane confirmed that Badrou Bouzar was not happy in his marital life. He became addicted to watching porn at night; during the daytime, too, even when he was in his office. The Colonel did not ask about the source of this piece of information, but he was convinced that his aide was not talking from nothing. He guessed that he had hacked into Badrou's computer and found something there.

He noticed that Ziane hadn't shared everything he knew. When hesitant and nervous, Ziane fiddled with his silver ring, repeatedly taking it off and putting it back on.

"Go on!" Soltani said, encouraging him to speak.

"I have pictures of Badrou Bouzar's secretary not wearing a hijab."

"So what if she's not wearing a hijab?"

"I mean, practically naked, sir."

"Really?!"

Samir reached over to the iPad and opened up the picture folder. After a few seconds, Amira Derbal appeared sporting short blond hair and very revealing underwear. The Colonel had no problem reconciling these pictures with the same veiled young woman he had met that morning. People were not always as they appeared.

He ordered his aide to add Amira Derbal's name to the list of persons of interest. She might be working with Badrou Bouzar.

Soltani's hunch was not wrong. He received a call from Amira Derbal fifteen minutes later, telling him that she knew where Badrou Bouzar was. He was hiding in an apartment he owned in Hamri that he used on rare occasions. Soltani thought that arresting Badrou would certainly help solve the puzzle of Hoopoe's murder. The initial clues were clear, and they all pointed to him. The time had come for him to stop dodging and confess. When Badrou had accused Falcon and the political cartoonist, Rachid Kadri, was that just a smoke screen? To buy some time and make a quick exit?

"Mr. Bouzar thinks his life is in danger and that he might be killed in the most awful way. Like what happened to Mr. Miloud Sabri," said Amira.

"Why?"

"I don't know...but he asked me to run away with him. He said he had some money stashed away in banks abroad and that we could live like royalty."

"What else?"

"I advised him to turn himself in, but he just replied that he had fallen into a well-constructed trap that he wouldn't get out of alive. That it was too late. And he kept saying, 'The dove has flown! The dove has flown!'"

Soltani asked her where she was. She told him that she was on her way to meet Badrou. He ordered her to wait for him there, and he would meet up with her right away. She gave him the address and begged him not to be late. He got up from his chair and headed out. Right then, Captain Ziane rushed in, saying, "I have significant information about the cocaine case, sir."

"I'm listening."

"One of Hoopoe's partners in the cocaine shipping business is someone we know well."

"Who's that?"

"Belkacemi."

"Our general?!"

"No, Tarik Belkacemi."

"The Boss's son?"

"That's the one."

"And the information is reliable?"

"Very reliable, sir."

Soltani thought about Tarik, who was no more than thirty-five before his star had risen in a constellation of corruption under the guise of "investments" in the last two years. Many of those like the General's son who call themselves "investors" don't use their capital. Rather, they work with their influence and connections. Investing in real estate and drugs is a typical leap in the history of all gangs, going back to the Sicilian Mafia. He made a quick decision not to inform General Belkacemi of this new information until he answered two questions: Was the General protecting his son? Was there a direct connection between the Boss and Miloud Sabri?

12

Spring, Summer, and Fall 1988

The cartoonist, Rachid Kadri, arrived half an hour before he was to meet one of his friends at the University of Oran in the Senia district, so he decided to kill some time in the library. Luckily, he found an empty seat. The place was packed. He sat flipping through a book by the Palestinian cartoonist, Naji al-Ali, filled with drawings of Handala, the heroic character the cartoonist had created to express the plight of the Palestinians. While Rachid was thinking about the unfortunate fate of Handala, who always had his back turned to everyone, he caught sight of a beautiful young woman with curly black hair sitting just across the corridor, not too far from him. She did not notice him sneaking looks at her, engrossed as she was reading, moving from one book to another like an energetic bee. He studied her for a few minutes, then reached into his bag, pulled out his pens and a notebook, and proceeded to draw her. He did this for a full hour without noticing the passage of time, completely forgetting about meeting his friend. He was very focused and usually drew quickly but did not understand what was going on. He drew and re-drew, unsatisfied with the results. This was serious!

"Where should I begin? The hair or the eyes? The lips or the nose?"

Suddenly, he saw her gather up her papers and books to leave. He thought about going up to her and asking for more time to finish the drawing but did not dare. He walked toward her, trying to come up with a pretext to talk with her. He heard her ask a library employee to hold on to some books she was not finished with yet, saying that she would return the following day to complete her assignment. Rachid took a deep breath and thanked God.

The beautiful girl left the library, and he followed. He guessed she was heading toward the main gate, and he was right. Just as she walked out, she met another student, and it appeared from the warmth of the greeting and how deeply they hugged that they had not seen one another in a long time. They chatted for more than five minutes, then said goodbye, and she continued on her way. Rachid followed her like an experienced security agent but could not enjoy the chase for too long because right then, a black Peugeot 405 pulled up next to her. He saw her open the door and get into the front seat. He looked at the car for a while but could only glean that the driver was a man.

"Who's the lucky guy?" he wondered.

He proceeded to weigh the possibilities. If it was her father or brother, he was still in luck. If it was her husband or fiancé, then he was as good as dead.

The next day, Rachid left the College of Fine Arts and hurried to the university library. He breathed a sigh of relief when he saw her exactly where she had been sitting the previous day, surrounded by her books and papers. He found a chair close to her that would give him a better view, then took out his tools and began to draw. After less than an hour, he saw her gather her things, which meant she was leaving.

"Please, not now," he mumbled.

He was overwhelmed with a strange feeling that he would never see her again, which meant he would never finish the drawing. What to do? He hesitated a little but quickly gathered up all his courage and love for challenges and took a chance. He walked up to her and said, "Excuse me, miss, I haven't finished my drawing."

"I'm sorry, what's that?"

"Please sit down so I can explain."

She hesitated before taking a seat and asking, "What do you want from me?"

Rachid's heart started to flutter, and he felt his hands shaking. He stammered, but in the nick of time, he thought of a ruse that would get him through this impasse. He told her that he was a student at the College of Fine Arts and that, in order to pass a difficult exam, he needed to submit a quality drawing. Serendipitously, he had found a suitable subject the previous day and needed a few minutes to complete the work. He apologized to her for not asking for permission first. She looked at him and asked, "I'm your subject?"

"That's right."

"Where's the drawing?"

"It's not done yet."

"Doesn't matter. I want to see it."

Rachid opened the notebook to the drawing. She looked at it for a moment, then lifted her eyes and said, "Who is this creature?"

"You."

"Why did you draw me like this? Shame on you!"

"I'm a cartoonist."

She placed her finger on the hooked nose and big lips in the drawing and started to laugh without regard for the people around them. Instead of trying to quiet her down, Rachid laughed along with her. After apologizing to those around her, she told him she was leaving because she was losing focus. It would be better for her to return tomorrow with more energy. He took the opportunity to invite her to a nearby cafeteria, and she agreed.

"She wouldn't have accepted my invitation if she were married. Is she engaged? Maybe yes, and maybe no," he thought to himself.

They sat across from one another and exchanged preliminary information. He learned her name was Souad, and she was in her first year in the Foreign Languages Department. They talked about general topics: Algeria's relationship to the Third World, the mixed blessing of petroleum, the housing crisis, the Palestinian issue, the fact that Oran was the most beautiful city in the Mediterranean, and so on and so forth. He listened to her, completely captivated, and she asked him many questions about the relationship between life and art, artists and madness.

When she got up to say goodbye, Rachid asked her, "When will we meet tomorrow?"

"Why?"

"I need to finish the drawing."

"Same time as today."

The following day, Souad Sabri arrived at the university library on time. Rachid Kadri was already there. He sat in front of her. There was no reason to hide this time, and he allowed himself to gaze at her as he wished, using the drawing as a pretext. From time to time, she would shyly raise her eyes. He finished the drawing but wanted to prolong the moment for as long as possible.

"Have you finished?" she asked, smiling.

"Yes, I have."

"I want a copy."

"No. I'll make you a new drawing."

Rachid sought to convince her that true art recognizes originals only, not copies, and that each drawing has its own unique characteristics.

They left the library and headed to the same cafeteria where they had sat the previous day. Rachid could not wait any longer, so he asked about her marital status. She smiled and said, "I'm not married and not officially engaged."

Rachid did not understand the word "officially," but he didn't press it.

He told her he was from Mascara and that it never bothered him when people from Oran made fun of those from Mascara. Not only was it nice to make someone laugh and bring them a little cheer, but he was proud of his roots. Mascara had given Algeria the hero of the anti-colonial resistance, Emir Abdelkader, the best player in the history of Algerian soccer, Lakhdar Belloumi, and the best red wine, Coteaux de Mascara.

Two months after meeting, he suggested they see an Italian movie at the Cinémathèque, and she agreed. He made the most of a romantic scene between Sofia Loren and Marcello Mastroianni and grabbed on to her hand. She pulled her hand away, but with just a bit of hesitation. This was encouraging, so he took three more stabs at it until she reciprocated. After the movie, they made their way toward the sea as Souad praised Italian romanticism. She told him about her numerous trips to Italy and how much she liked Florence. Rachid waited for the right moment, afforded by that Italian atmosphere and the romance surrounding it, and cast his hook.

"Do you know how an Algerian man says 'I love you' to his beloved?"

"'I love you as I love my own eyes.'"

"That's how they say it in Egyptian soap operas!"

"Then tell me."

"'I love you, God damnit!'"

Rachid said the words spiritedly and forcefully, and Souad started to laugh, as did he. Then, she remarked on the reasons why Algerians lacked romance. He asked her not to generalize. There were romantic Algerians who were no less romantic than the Italians. She responded that while there were always exceptions, they were rare. Right then, he grabbed her hand and looked into her eyes.

"I love you, Souad."

"Are you sure?"

"I love you, Souad... I love you, God damnit!"

"You're one hundred percent Algerian!"

They started laughing again. Souad was just about to tell him she loved him as well, but shyness prevented her from doing so.

Youssef Misbah called his brother-in-law, Miloud Sabri, in the morning and asked to see him immediately. He insisted they meet somewhere other than home. Hoopoe understood that it had to do with sensitive family matters, so he arranged to see him in his office that evening. Youssef was indebted to Hoopoe for everything; if not for him, he would not have risen to the military rank of captain so quickly.

"We have a problem with Souad."

"What did she do, Brother Youssef?"

"She's fallen in love with someone from Mascara, dirt poor..."

"People will laugh at us, brother."

"She's still a child," said Youssef.

"I already gave my word, and it would be shameful to go back on it."

"You're right."

"Can you take care of this, Brother Youssef?"

"Of course."

"But you have to hide it from your sister."

"Understood."

Souad was always a source of contention between her parents. Hoopoe was unable to tame her or wrap her around his finger as he had with her older sister, Mona.

Souad completely rebelled and rejected outright the idea of marrying the son of a general. Dolores stood with her, and Hoopoe did not want to clash with his wife. Hoopoe was sure he could use his cunning to convince the two of them together. But Dolores promised her daughter that she would marry who *she* wanted to marry, not who her father chose.

The following day, Youssef Misbah intervened personally to solve the problem. Rachid Kadri was returning to his house in Medina Jedida when a black car stopped in front of him. He was immediately surrounded. One of the men said, "Come with us."

"Who are you?"

"Military Security."

Rachid got into the car and found himself next to Captain Youssef Misbah, who was smoking a Gauloise cigarette. He smiled as he said, "Hello, Romeo."

"What do you want from me?"

"Aren't you ashamed? Running around like a dog after married women."

"You've got it all wrong," replied Rachid.

"We're never wrong, you son of a bitch!" Youssef slapped him hard.

Then, he pulled some pictures out of an envelope of Rachid with Souad. Most of the pictures were taken in the university cafeteria. Rachid looked both astonished and surprised. In a menacing voice, Youssef said, "Stay away from this fine girl, for your own good."

"Souad isn't married."

"Whether she's married or engaged is none of your business."

They let him out of the car, followed by a series of high-caliber insults.

Two days later, Souad met Rachid at the university. He was not his usual cheerful self. She asked him how he was, and he could not keep what had happened from her. He gave her the details and described the Gauloise-smoking security officer. She had no difficulty figuring out who he was.

"The messenger was my Uncle Youssef."

"And who sent him?"

"My father... Miloud Sabri."

"Souad, tell me the truth."

"What do you want to know?"

"Are you engaged?"

"My father gave his word to someone without consulting me first, but I refused."

"Why is he forcing you to get married?"

This question opened the door to many topics. She told him her sad story with Hoopoe and how he sought to tame her as if she were a horse. If not for her mother, who supported her, she would not have been able to resist and live her life. Souad didn't notice the tears as they streamed down her cheeks.

"I love you, Rachid. Don't leave me."

"I won't leave you, Souad."

"Do you swear?"

"I swear... I love you, God damnit."

She held back her tears and began to smile. Then she started to laugh.

When Souad got home, her mother could see she was upset. She knew something was up and asked her what had happened. Souad could no longer keep it a secret. She told her all about her love affair with Rachid, from the first time they met in the university library until her Uncle Youssef's threats.

That same week, Hoopoe went to France for five days to buy a new car, and Dolores invited her brother over for dinner. After eating, Youssef rushed to light a Gauloise as they sat together in the living room. He could only fully enjoy lunch or dinner if it was followed by a cigarette. He knew well that his sister's way of broaching sensitive topics was completely different than that of her husband. She got right to the heart of the matter, leaving no room for surprises or misunderstandings.

"Tell me, Youssef. If, God forbid, my husband and I disagreed about something, whose side would you choose?"

"God forbid!"

"Who would you choose, Youssef?"

"Where is this coming from?"

"You don't want to answer, is that it? Listen up, Youssef, stay away from Souad and Rachid."

"As you like, sister."

She hoped that Youssef understood the message well and that he would no longer involve himself in her daughter's business. He could not aim to satisfy Hoopoe at her expense. Youssef had been afraid of his sister since he was young. Her participation in guerrilla operations left the impression that if she wanted to harm someone, nothing would stand in her way.

Captain Youssef Misbah and his brother-in-law, Hoopoe, followed President Chadli Bendjedid's speech, which was broadcast on television. The President called on the people to rebel against bureaucracy and corruption and to stand with him in the name of reform. He sent several coded messages, but the poor people did not understand what he meant. The amazing thing was that the President spoke as if he were a political opponent of his own regime.

"The flood is coming, Brother Youssef."

"And Noah's ark is ready."

"Algeria needs to walk a different path."

"And it *will* walk a different path. Scorners will scorn, and haters will hate," said Youssef enthusiastically.

Hoopoe was not wrong in his assessments. The flood really did come on October 5. Young people shed their fears and lit fires in the Liberation Front Party headquarters. In response, the oppression machine revved up. The army intervened and fired on defenseless citizens.

On the night of October 9, while the cartoonist Rachid Kadri was speaking with Souad on the phone, he heard a loud knocking at the door. He asked her to hold on. As soon as he opened the door, two people fell on him and beat him up. Rachid looked up and saw Youssef Misbah's men, whom he had met before. Souad's uncle was not there. They handcuffed him, put a dirty sack over his head, and shoved him into a car. The driver took off at a crazy speed, and every once in a while, they would punch him in the face or the stomach just for fun, as a warm-up.

After about fifteen minutes, the car stopped. They yanked him out and ordered him to walk. He fell down multiple times, enduring insults and punches, his nose bleeding. He heard the sound of a door open, then close. They undid the handcuffs and took the sack off his head. He found himself in a small, lit room full of people. They all looked like they had been beaten up. As he took his leave, one of Youssef Misbah's men said, "Welcome. We will provide the hospitality the situation requires, you son of a bitch." He followed his words up with a punch that knocked him to the ground.

An hour later, a person called him by name and ordered him to go with him. Rachid walked behind him up to the second floor, where he was placed in a windowless room. There, he saw a young man lying in his own blood on the floor. It appeared that he had lost consciousness after receiving his share of torture at the hands of four people. After waiting for a few minutes, their boss arrived. They called him "Pharaoh," and he gave the green light to start the party. They grabbed Rachid like a sheep on Eid and stripped him of his clothing. Punches and kicks rained down on him from all sides. He tried to protect his face, but it was no use.

He got a taste of various kinds of torture that ranged from drinking urine to beating to electrocution. He figured out a trick that granted him a bit of rest and stopped the torture machine for a few minutes; he would pretend to lose consciousness, which would cause their conductor to stop the music. Perhaps they were afraid he would give up the ghost before they had had enough of their party.

That evening, a person escorted him to the fourth floor, where there were offices rather than torture chambers. The person knocked on the door and had him enter. Rachid went in and saw the Pharaoh sitting on a comfortable sofa. He stood up and extended his hand to welcome him. Rachid hesitated a bit before shaking his hand. The Pharaoh smiled and offered him a cigarette, which Rachid accepted without hesitation. He was in desperate need of one. He thought the Pharaoh was just playing a game. Perhaps he thought that the carrot might work where the stick had not. Rachid did not have any prior experience with torture and torturers, so he did not know how it worked. As time passed, the Pharaoh became increasingly polite, which completely baffled Rachid.

"Coffee?"

"No... What do you want with me?"

"We only want what's best, Mr. Kadri."

Rachid did not understand a thing he was saying, but the Pharaoh did not beat around the bush for too long. He told him that orders had been issued from above to let him go immediately. Rachid left that hellhole bruised, swollen, and in pain but intact. He could not believe it.

"Had they gotten the name wrong and let me go? If it wasn't that, then what happened?"

What happened was that when Rachid was taken from his apartment, he was with one of his friends, who told Souad. Souad then rushed to tell her mother so she could rescue her lover. Dolores called up her brother, Youssef, who realized that she was placing the responsibility on him. Fifteen minutes later, Youssef called her back and told her that one of his enthusiastic and fawning aides had acted without consulting him first because he wanted to ingratiate himself with him. The aide realized that the arrest campaign targeting protestors was a valuable opportunity to teach Rachid a lesson he would not forget. Youssef ordered Rachid be released immediately, and his orders were carried out without delay.

That night, Dolores saw her daughter smiling and cheerful and knew that her knight had been freed. Souad rushed forward and hugged her.

Driss Talbi, aka Falcon, had joined a group of lawyers, doctors, and intellectuals to create a working group that would document testimonies of citizens who were tortured in October 1988. He met Rachid through Souad. Falcon remarked that he had not expected the regime to be transformed into a rabid dog that would take a bite out of the Algerian people. They had risen up against colonialism and oppression, but had they achieved their goal? Had they regained their freedom? He was enraged by the issue of torture, so he screamed again and again, "We freed the country, but we didn't free the people!"

Nabil Talbi always celebrated his mother's birthday alone. He would visit her grave in Aïn Al-Baida Cemetery, bringing her roses and reciting the opening verses of the Qur'an over her spirit. Then, he would return home and spend the rest of the day recalling beautiful memories of her. He would cry and renew his vow year after year: “Whoever deprived me of you will not escape punishment, my dear mother.”

13

Thursday, July 5, 2018

5:19 P.M.

Colonel Karim Soltani parked his car in front of a new building near Ahmed Zabana Stadium. He took out his small notebook to check on the address that Badrou Bouzar's secretary, Amira Derbal, had given him. He glanced in his rearview mirror and saw a gray car stopped not far from him. First Lieutenant Malika Derraji was in the driver's seat, and Captain Samir Ziane was sitting next to her. The Colonel followed protocol in such cases and did not come alone, for arresting Badrou might not be easy. He might be with his accomplices. Anything was possible, and it was necessary to take all precautions. He got out of the car and glanced around quickly, but there was no sign of the beautiful secretary. He wondered why she was late for the appointment, so he called her at the number she had given him. The line was busy.

Soltani lit a cigarette to ease some of the stress of waiting. He looked to the other side of the street and saw a large blue sign: "Renault 1949." He guessed it was a car repair shop that seemed to have been closed for some time—so many lingering traces evoking the French presence in this city's neighborhoods, and no wonder. Oran was a European city par excellence, unlike other Algerian cities where Europeans were a minority. Its fate has been tied to Europe since the beginning. Andalusian sailors established it in 902. Then, it was passed from the Fatimids to the Umayyads to the Almoravids to the Almohads to the Zayyanids to the Marinids to the Hafsids. The city fell into Spanish hands in 1509, and the Ottomans wrested it from them in 1708. Twenty-four years later, the Spanish got it back. The second occupation only lasted sixty years when a devastating earthquake forced the Spanish forces to withdraw and hand Oran over to Mohamed ben Othmane Bey, better known as Mohamed the Great. The Ottomans remained in the city until it fell to the French in January 1831.

Ten minutes later, Soltani saw a white Renault Clio pull up. Amira Derbal got out and rushed over. She apologized for being late without providing any explanation. He tried to put the pictures of her in sexy lingerie out of his mind.

"Do you know this place?"

"No, this is my first time here, Colonel."

"Is Badrou Bouzar here alone?"

"God only knows."

The Colonel raised his hand in some sort of a signal, the meaning of which Amira did not understand until a second later when she saw two young people standing in front of her. She realized who they were when Soltani began to issue orders. They worked with him. He ordered Derraji to accompany him to Badrou Bouzar's apartment. As for Ziane, he charged him with staying out in front of the building with Amira to keep an eye out, ready to intervene if necessary.

He walked up to the second floor with his aide, avoiding the elevator. After ringing the doorbell more than once with no sign of life, he started knocking hard. At that moment, a young man in his thirties burst out of the apartment next door. The Colonel did not give him any time to vent his anger and informed him that he was from Anti-Terrorism. The neighbor asked to see some identification so he could be sure. Soltani realized that the individual was not an ordinary civilian. He showed his card, and the young man gave him a crisp military salute. The Colonel did not ask for his rank or which branch of the military he served in, but he tried to get information from him about his neighbor. The fellow said that Hadj Badrou did not come to this apartment too much and that he was a blessing of a neighbor. He lavished him with the most wonderful praise, so much that the Colonel pictured Badrou Bouzar as a holy saint. Hadj Badrou! Had he made the pilgrimage to Mecca? There was no doubt. He wondered what the neighbor's reaction would be if he saw what Badrou did on the internet. Would he still call him "Hadj"?

He asked the neighbor if he could use the balcony to reach Badrou's place, and the neighbor agreed immediately, even offering to help. Soltani thanked him and told him he would not hesitate to ask for help if necessary. The Colonel asked his aide to remain in front of the apartment door. Soltani deftly climbed the short wall separating the two balconies onto Badrou Bouzar's balcony. He looked inside through the main window and saw Badrou's body on the floor. He broke the window and went in, gun drawn. Badrou's lifeless corpse lay there. He felt for a pulse and confirmed that he was gone. He looked to the right and found a broken glass, which appeared to have fallen from his hand and smashed on the floor. He opened the apartment door for Derraji, who had her gun drawn and was ready to strike. He told her that Badrou was dead. They carefully searched the three-room apartment but did not find anyone.

The Colonel telephoned Ziane and asked him to come up and to bring Amira Derbal with him. A few minutes later, Ziane came in, with Amira following behind. As soon as she saw Badrou's lifeless body on the floor, she screamed, "The poor man killed himself!"

"How do you know?" asked Soltani.

"He drank poison. He was afraid of being slaughtered like his father-in-law, Mr. Miloud Sabri."

The Colonel called the medical examiner, Abdou Hamlaoui, and asked him to come immediately. He told him that there was a second body awaiting him today. He wanted to confirm it was suicide by poisoning. But did he commit suicide, or was he killed? Amira was sobbing. Derraji tried to console her, but it was no use. Suddenly, Amira rushed to the toilet as if she was about to throw up. Derraji went in behind her.

After a short while, Amira returned, but she was still crying. Soltani asked her to calm down and tell him what Badrou had said to her the last time they spoke. He urged her to include everything. She stopped crying and sighed. Then she said he had called her an hour before in a state of utter terror. From the tone of his voice, she felt like he was shaking. She tried to reassure him, but all her attempts failed. She suggested he turn himself in, but he refused. He was in too deep and would not get out alive. The only solution was to leave the country without delay.

Soltani let the secretary talk, waiting for her to utter a piece of important information that might help him solve Badrou's murder. He was not convinced of the suicide theory at all. Badrou was not a weak person. He was trained in hardship. Working as an agent with the security forces all these years had not been easy, especially in the '90s. A person like him wouldn't give up like this without first playing all his cards. Every agent hides a winning card (or more than one) to play when absolutely necessary. Those who work with the security apparatuses are never cut off from the tree. He must have had a web of connections, friendships, and mutual interests that he had worked hard to spin and maintain. Badrou was an expert dealmaker, and he possessed considerable wealth. "Money can pave a road in the sea," as the saying goes. Why didn't he use his cards then? What happened to him?

"Who was Badrou afraid of?" asked Soltani.

"Of the Libyans who killed Mr. Miloud, sir."

"Who told you that?"

"Mr. Bouzar."

"Did he give a reason?"

"An arms deal gone bad. An unknown party got involved and ruined the deal by replacing working weapons with faulty ones during the shipment."

"Who was the unknown party?"

"God only knows, sir."

"When did he tell you this?"

"This morning."

"You know all of his secrets!"

"No, that's not true."

"Why don't you tell the truth?" Soltani said angrily.

"I swear, I don't know."

"What was your relationship with Badrou Bouzar?"

"I don't understand."

"I mean... were you just a secretary or...?" he said sternly.

"How dare you!" she said as she started to cry again.

Soltani left the apartment and went next door. The soldier opened the door before he knocked, as if he had been watching through the peephole. He gestured to him and asked, "Did you see anyone visit Badrou Bouzar today?"

"Three hours ago, I saw a man go in, sir."

"How did he enter?"

"Hadj Badrou opened the door for him, sir."

"Could you describe him for me?"

"I can't. I didn't see his face. I just saw him from behind, sir."

"What about the clothes?"

"The person was wearing a black tracksuit and a hat, but I don't remember what color."

Soltani considered the possibility that the person who visited Badrou might have been one of the people who had killed Hoopoe. This based on what his aide, Derraji, had told him about the security cameras revealing two people fitting that same description close to the Mistress's Villa.

Twenty minutes later, the medical examiner, Abdou Hamlaoui, arrived. Even though he was in his mid-sixties, he had jet-black hair, which everyone thought he might dye. Many had placed bets on it, but no one could confirm or refute it. It remained shrouded in mystery. Dr. Hamlaoui greeted everyone there and smiled at Soltani.

"Two murders in one day, God forbid."

"And the best may be yet to come," Soltani responded.

The medical examiner began to examine the corpse and the broken glass carefully. After a few minutes, he had come to a couple of conclusions. The deceased most likely died of poisoning with strychnine; the blueness of the tongue was proof of that. As for whether it was murder or suicide, the deceased might have taken the poison by himself, given the fact that the glass had fallen and broken on the floor. No way of knowing why. Did he kill himself, or did he drink the poison without knowing? This seemed like a good question to the Colonel. Perhaps someone had poisoned him, then locked the door behind them and left. Amira was listening to the conversation. Derraji turned to her and asked, "Have you been to this apartment before?"

"No, never."

"This is the first time?"

"Yes, the first time," answered Amira.

Derraji pulled the Colonel aside and, in a hushed tone, informed him that the secretary was lying. She knew Amira had visited this apartment before because she had observed her moving around comfortably, going to the bathroom, and then to the kitchen to get a glass of water from one of the shelves. It was clear that the secretary was familiar with the apartment. Why was she lying? Was she afraid it would damage her reputation? Was she Badrou's mistress? The pictures of her confirmed that. Was she working alone, or was she part of a gang? Who were her partners?

Soltani decided to be patient with the secretary and not show his cards just yet, especially not concerning the pictures. There was no reason to arrest her now. Perhaps she had made some sort of mistake. He told her she could go and that he would call her if he needed to. Amira's face relaxed, which only increased his suspicions. What was she hiding? There were many open questions. Amira was not just a secretary. She played other roles as well. Perhaps she ate at more than one table. The Colonel thought that some research into her life might help solve Badrou Bouzar's murder and perhaps Hoopoe's as well. Amira was smart, and he mustn't underestimate her.

After Amira left, he ordered his aide, Ziane, to follow her and listen in on her telephone calls. Perhaps she would contact her partners soon.

Soltani realized that the time had come to bring the Boss into the picture, so he called him to tell him the good news: two murders on the same day!

"Oh, God. What a horrible day!" the General said.

"Don't say that about blessed Independence Day, sir."

"Oh, good God, don't provoke me. So far, we have many clues about the Libyan theory."

"The Libyan theory is baseless."

"Listen to me, Soltani... at least we have a bone we can give to..."

"To who? Who do you mean, sir?"

General Belkacemi hung up without answering the question.

14

Winter and Spring 1992

Badrou Bouzar got to Hoopoe's office just before their appointment, wet from the rain. He had received a call from him asking him to come before eight that evening. Hoopoe did not tell him why, but he insisted that Badrou not be even one minute late. When he entered, Badrou found Hoopoe reclining on the sofa, staring at the television. He tried to ask him what the hurry was, but Hoopoe indicated to him to be quiet and sit down. After a few seconds, the news broadcast started, and the President of the Republic, Chadli Bendjedid, was submitting his resignation to members of the Constitutional Council. Immediately after that, the announcer read the text of the resignation speech. The last bit was particularly moving:

> That is why, brothers, sisters, and fellow citizens, as of today, I relinquish the duties of President of the Republic, and I ask each and every one of us to consider

this decision a sacrifice on my part for the sake of the nation's greater good.

Long live Algeria! Glory and eternity to our martyrs!

Badrou was tense. As for Hoopoe, he was delighted and in the mood to talk.

"Resignation is the safest exit for him and the country."

"But, the Islamists will wreck havoc, Uncle Miloud!"

"What can they do?"

"They can call for jihad."

"In words."

"And... deeds."

"What do they have?"

"They won the elections. The people are with them."

"The people are with whoever is left standing. The Islamists are like a sheep," laughed Hoopoe.

He took out a Cuban cigar and wet it between his lips before carefully clipping off the end. He called for God's mercy on the soul of President Boumediene. Thanks to him, he was a lover of Cuban cigars. Then he explained things to Badrou in the simplest possible terms. Essentially, the Eid sheep starts off as a small animal that cannot live without being nursed. Then it gets stronger and starts to eat straw. Little by little, it sprouts horns on its head, which quickly grow and become a means of defending itself. In the end, the animal can be used for two things: You can put it in the ring to butt heads and frighten animals and people, and then you can slaughter it on the morning of Eid al-Adha to enjoy its grilled flesh and make the children happy. What's surprising is that the sheep is driven to the slaughterhouse without it ever suspecting a thing. This is the role and fate of the Islamists, like the Muslim Brotherhood in Egypt, who were exploited by King Farouk and then thrown into prisons. After that, Nasser rode them to success in overthrowing the king and then getting rid of Mohammed Naguib. Finally, he arrested and tortured them, even hanging some of them.

Hoopoe lit his cigar and looked at Badrou with a complicit smile.

"Do you understand the Eid sheep theory now, Badrou?"

"I understand, Uncle Miloud."

"Now we have definitive proof that Imam Khomeini's experiment will not repeat itself in Algeria."

"Why not?"

"The army doesn't want to share power—neither with the Islamists nor with anyone else."

"So what's the next expected scenario, Uncle Miloud?"

"It's a work in progress," Hoopoe said with a wink.

Badrou left Hoopoe's office thinking about the Eid sheep theory. He thought back to the post–October 1988 period and began to piece things together. Hoopoe was among those who enthusiastically supported amendments to the constitution in February 1989, which opened the way for a multiparty system and the end of the Liberation Front Party's governing monopoly.

During that time, Badrou closely followed discussions among leaders of the Islamist trend. There were two opposing camps. One side opposed participating in the political game at all costs under the pretext that democracy was blasphemy. The other side supported participation in politics not out of a belief in democracy but rather in order not to leave the chair empty for their secular and communist opponents to fill. And when they grabbed hold of the reins of power, well, they would cross that bridge when they came to it. Badrou pointed out that the law related to political parties did not allow the establishment of parties based on language or religion. Hoopoe responded that the government was weak at the moment. That it was necessary to strike while the iron was hot. He then elaborated on how the Islamist movement inside the Liberation Front had managed in just a few years to turn the tables on the leftists and the socialists. This was evidenced by the Family Law of 1984, which was supported by Islamic Sharia law, especially in relation to divorce. It granted men many privileges, and many factions in the Liberation Front Party were prepared to join a strong Islamic party. After the first Islamic party in the country was established, Hoopoe laughed at the new party's name: Le Front Islamique du Salut (Islamic Salvation Front). The acronym of the French name was FIS, pronounced like the French word "fils," meaning "son." He said to Badrou, smiling, "May God bless the Front's family."

"And protect it from all enemies."

"The Salvation Front is the Liberation Front's son."

"Standing on the shoulders of giants, Uncle Miloud."

"You're so right," Hoopoe said, unleashing a thunderous laugh that Badrou quickly imitated.

The Islamists backed Badrou as a candidate for the municipal elections in 1990, but he politely declined, following Hoopoe's advice to avoid drawing attention to himself. He justified his position by saying that there were people more deserving than he. They took his refusal as a sign of modesty, and some of them said repeatedly, "He who humbles himself to God is raised up by Him. You're a good Muslim, Brother Badrou."

Badrou Bouzar learned many lessons during his friendly association with Hoopoe, the most important of which, by far, was to avoid the front lines. In wars, soldiers die on the front lines. As for the leaders, they issue orders far from the action. Hoopoe could have taken all the positions he wanted but always refused. Whenever he was offered something, he thanked whoever was thinking of him and suggested someone else. And when his role as middleman succeeded, the person he had elevated would be forever in his debt. This is how he was able to create a vast network of "partners," as he liked to call them.

He continued to play both sides. He bet on the Islamists finding the same success they did in the Iranian Revolution. He encouraged, from behind the scenes, of course, the civil disobedience waged by the Islamic Salvation Front against President Bendjedid and the government of Hamrouche in the summer of 1991. The consequences were dire when the army intervened again, following the precedent of October 1988, to put a stop to the disobedience and sit-ins in the public squares. Following that, two Islamist leaders, Abbassi Madani and Ali Benhadj, were arrested. Then, at the end of December 1991, the results of the legislative elections surprised everyone. The Islamists won nearly half of the seats in parliament in the first round and were poised to gain more seats in the second round, thereby controlling the government. However, the army decided to cancel the elections and establish the High Council of State, which consisted of five members headed by one of the revolution's leaders, Mohamed Boudiaf, known as Si Tayeb, his nom de guerre during the War of Independence.

Hoopoe and his brother-in-law, Youssef Misbah, followed the inaugural ceremonies on live television of the Chairman of the High Council of State, Mohamed Boudiaf, who enjoyed a hero's welcome. The line of soldiers and civilians welcoming him was long. Boudiaf doled out a great many kisses, and in the VIP lounge at the airport, he made some bold statements, including an announcement that the Liberation Front Party's role had ended in 1962 and that it was time to put it to rest. Hoopoe could not understand Boudiaf: Why would he reject the alliance with the army in 1962 and then accept it thirty years later? The army had changed. Algeria had changed. The people had changed. The world had changed.

"Why didn't Boudiaf stay in Morocco and enjoy his life with his kids and grandkids?" wondered Hoopoe, a bit confused.

Driss Talbi, aka Falcon, met with Mohamed Boudiaf as part of a delegation of lawyers during a visit to the President of the Republic. Boudiaf seemed enthusiastic and sincere, determined to fight what he called the political and economic mafia. However, enthusiasm, sincerity, and determination are useless without knowing how the government actually operates. Falcon came out of that meeting pessimistic and dejected. He could not understand some of the security decisions Boudiaf supported, such as arresting thousands of Islamic Salvation Front fighters and sending them to prisons in the south. Boudiaf's statement to the press shocked him: "If it is necessary to send tens of thousands of people to camps in the south for a specific period of time in order to save Algeria, then the choice is simple. I say that without feeling the slightest bit guilty."

"Was Boudiaf in his right mind? He seems to have completely forgotten about his arrest and imprisonment in the south in 1963 under President Ahmed Ben Bella," remarked Falcon incredulously.

After Chadli's resignation, the cancellation of legislative elections, the imposition of emergency law, and the dissolution of the Islamic Salvation Front, many innocent people were arrested, including Falcon's neighbor's son, whom he had known since he was a boy. The young man was a good student at the university; his only mistake was joining a legal political party—one that was recognized by the state, participated in the elections, and won them by the Interior Minister's own admission!

It was Falcon's habit to ask three questions in his private meetings: Whose interests are being served in transforming this party into something so terrifying? Who is convinced, deluded even, that *his* fighters are the strongest and that they might easily gain control? How had they fallen into the trap so quickly?

The latest developments were not only on the political level. The truth surrounding the tragedy of Abbas Badi, aka Stork, had begun to emerge. Stork was accused of betraying his superior, Yazid, during the war, and he was punished by having his nose cut off. A man came to Driss Talbi's office and requested to see him immediately. He was a comrade of Cherif Miqdad, the unfortunate veteran freedom fighter who had told him in 1976 that his late wife, Farida, was the one who had betrayed Yazid. Miqdad had been found slain outside his apartment, taking a huge secret with him to the grave.

After a bit of back-and-forth, Falcon learned that the man had also been one of Omar's men and was suffering from lung cancer. His days were numbered. He came to absolve himself before God and His servants in the case of Abbas Badi. He was prepared to tell the whole truth without any fear of reprisal. He was not at all concerned with the consequences. He had nothing to lose.

"A day before he was killed, Cherif Miqdad told me that he revealed the mistress's name to you."

"That is correct," responded Falcon.

"And that he was hesitant to reveal the name of the traitor."

"That's also true. Do you know the traitor's name?" he asked eagerly.

"You also know it."

"I don't like riddles."

"He's your friend."

"Who?"

"Hoopoe."

"Miloud Sabri?!"

"That's right."

Falcon tried to pull himself together so as not to lose focus.

"Why have you kept quiet about this for all these years?"

"Hoopoe is the one who killed my friend, and he could kill me too."

"That's a serious accusation. Where's the proof? Were you present at Omar's meeting with Hoopoe?"

"Yes, but I was hiding."

"What do you mean?"

"Hoopoe asked Omar to keep the meeting a secret, but Omar didn't trust him, so he ordered us, Cherif Miqdad and me, to go with him and watch things from where Hoopoe couldn't see us."

Falcon drew on his experience investigating, practicing, and administering the law and asked the man whether he was prepared to face Hoopoe. He responded without hesitation that he was fully prepared to do that. The most he could hope for was to die a quick and painless death. Falcon tried to verify the details by asking more questions. The answers were coherent and persuasive, and Falcon concluded he was telling the truth. He would not gain anything from lying and accusing Hoopoe of wrongdoing. He aimed to tell the truth and rid himself of this heavy burden.

Stork was surprised when he opened his door the following day and found Falcon standing in front of him. He had not told him, as he usually did, that he was coming to visit. Falcon was nervous and unburdened himself as he stood there. Stork was silent for a moment. Then he started to cry. Falcon drew close and embraced him, and he began to cry too. Stork got up from his chair and left the house. Falcon understood that his friend needed to be alone. He came back an hour later, and Falcon asked him, "What do we do with this bastard Hoopoe?"

"Nothing," replied Stork.

"What?!"

"We do nothing."

"We have to kill him."

"When the time is right."

"What do you mean?"

Stork explained his position clearly, stating that he wanted to kill the traitor Hoopoe in front of God and all his servants. He wanted everyone to know that he was the killer. This was the only way he could restore his honor. However, if he killed him now, Dolores would know for sure, which would greatly harm her. He did not want to burden her with the scandal. Stork swore that when Dolores died, Hoopoe would follow the very next day. Then, he brought out a Qur'an and asked Falcon to swear he would not reveal the secret to anyone. Falcon became angry and accused him of cowardice. Then he calmed down and swore on it. He already knew he would be unable to convince him otherwise, no matter how hard he tried. As he was leaving, he asked, "Do you still love Dolores?"

"Her love is tattooed on my heart."

Hoopoe sat at the dinner table, surrounded by his wife, Dolores, his brother-in-law, Youssef, and his two daughters, Mona and Souad. Hoopoe recounted what had happened with Falcon. Earlier that day, Falcon had come to his office, seething, and said to him in a firm voice, "I don't ever want to see you again."

"Why, brother?"

"I'm not your brother," Falcon hissed.

"Tell me why?"

"You and I both know."

"What do you mean?"

"I told you... You and I both know, Hoopoe."

In the days that followed, Nabil, Dolores, and Souad tried to fix things between the two men, but it was no use. They tried to get an explanation but were shocked by Falcon's silence. Hoopoe commented on their failure to successfully mediate by saying, "I told you, there's no other explanation. He's lost his mind."

15

Thursday, July 5, 2018

7:14 P.M.

Colonel Karim Soltani parked in front of Badrou Bouzar's luxury villa in Nakhil, one of Oran's most exclusive neighborhoods. Amazed, he thought, "My God, how things have changed! A poor son from Sidi El Bachir becomes a billionaire in just a few years. How did that happen? What is the recipe for success, Badrou? Even if there were a recipe, no doubt it's as secret as Coca-Cola's. Wasn't it the poet, Moufdi Zakaria, who said, 'Algeria, the source of miracles'? And Badrou is overwhelming proof of that. From Sidi El Bachir to Nakhil...Long live Algeria!"

He rang the doorbell, and a policeman gripping a Kalashnikov opened the door for him. Then he was surprised by three armed policemen in the garden, looking like they were about to undertake a raid. He found two women in mourning clothes when he entered the living room. He had met the first one already and guessed that the second one was Mona, the newest arrival to the widows' club.

"What a horrible day, Colonel," cried Dolores.

"May God reward you, Madame Dolores."

He apologized for coming under such sad circumstances, but he desperately needed to connect the dots between the two crimes. Dolores replied that she understood and that he was just doing what he had to do. Mona remained silent. Every so often, she looked up. Her face was pale, streaked with tears and worry. Her blond hair had been ruined by repeated dye jobs. Suddenly, Mona broke her silence as if bitten by a viper. Fighting back her tears, she said, "I'm scared, Mother."

"Don't be scared, my girl."

"They'll kill us all."

"Who will kill you all, Madame Mona?" asked the Colonel, seeking an explanation with a bit of surprise.

"Whoever killed my father and my husband."

"And who is that?"

"They say they came from Libya," responded Mona.

Dolores hugged her daughter, who had retreated into silence and started crying again. Then she turned to the Colonel and told him that someone close to the family had visited them an hour before and revealed some dangerous information: There were hired assassins with a list of targets. They started with Hoopoe, then Badrou, and planned to kill their families too. The motive was payback for a deal that didn't go through. The Libyan gang that sent the killers wanted to be heard loud and clear, and for this to serve as a warning to anyone tempted to cheat and betray them. Anyone who went back on their promise and did not respect past agreements and pledges would be rewarded, them and their family, with gruesome murder. The message would be clear to all.

Dolores mentioned that she had asked for forces to be deployed to protect her and her family in the event of an emergency. She also contacted important people in the government to urge them to help prevent what happened to her husband and son-in-law from happening again.

Soltani declined to comment. He let the widowed mother finish, then asked, "Who gave you this information?"

"A relative."

"Your brother, Youssef Misbah?"

"No."

"May I know who it is?"

"Nabil Talbi."

"The journalist?!"

"Yes."

"Are you serious, madame?!"

He hid his displeasure and held his tongue as he wondered how journalists had become experts in security, terrorism, and crime. They even possessed state secrets. He reviewed the Libyan theory and emphasized that it drew inspiration from movies and stories about the mafia and organized crime. Scenarios cooked up in the imagination that are entirely divorced from reality. It was likely that Hoopoe's murder was connected to Badrou's. Were the two of them killed by the same hand? But the method of killing was different; Hoopoe was slaughtered, whereas Badrou was poisoned.

The widowed daughter started to wail louder, so Dolores asked if she could go with her to her room so she could calm down. He thanked the two widows and repeated his sincere condolences.

He left unsatisfied with what he had learned. The idea of assassins-for-hire coming from Libya had not entered his mind. Why was it being pushed? When he settled into the driver's seat, he wanted to make sure. He called a Libyan colleague he knew from the '90s, when the Algerian and Libyan armies were cooperating in the fight against terrorism. Two years ago, he was appointed military attaché at the Libyan embassy in Algeria. The Colonel refrained from discussing specific details of the case, only mentioning that Hoopoe had been threatened with death. He asked what the Libyan official thought. To him, it seemed unlikely that a group of armed assassins would be hired to liquidate Algerians, and on Algerian soil, no less. He summarized the reasons in two points: First, militias are more interested in winning battles inside Libya. They do not yet have sufficient strength to export their operations abroad. Secondly, Algeria was important to the Libyans, and it would not be in the interests of either side to make enemies. The Libyan did confirm that Hoopoe was involved in selling weapons to terrorists through Mali.

"According to my information, though, Hoopoe's role was marginal," the Libyan official said.

"So who holds the principal role?"

"His relative."

"Badrou Bouzar?"

"No, his wife's brother."

"Youssef Misbah?!"

"That's the one."

He thanked his Libyan colleague and hoped they would meet again soon. He then called his aide, Captain Ziane, and asked him to look into Youssef Misbah and Nabil Talbi. Ziane replied that he already had what was needed about the latter. The Colonel did not wish to inquire about sources. It is inappropriate to ask a computer hacker to reveal their sources or the ins and outs of how they operate. He asked his aide to wait for him in the office.

What Ziane kept to himself and tried to hide from everyone was that he had the ability to hack into the computers and email accounts of every public and private newspaper editor. They often possess very valuable information. Everyone adheres to a specific rule: Not everything known is published. Or, as the saying goes, "Check how deep the water is before crossing a river." Before any news item can be published, it is necessary to call friends in high places and seek their guidance. These folks don't want any trouble, and every one of them is out to cover his own ass.

The Colonel started the engine and headed back to the office. A few minutes later, he received a call from his aide, First Lieutenant Malika Derraji.

"I have information on the cocaine gang, sir."

"What's up?"

"A person living in Spain acted as a middleman in the deal. His name might interest you."

"Who is it?"

"Shaaban Alili, sir."

Of course, Derraji was aware of the situation involving Meriem's ex-husband. Before running off to Spain a year ago, he had made Meriem's life a living hell. He had threatened and tormented her, so the Colonel decided to confront him and solve the problem before it turned into a full-blown disaster. He had called him up, and they agreed to meet at the café in the Meridien Hotel.

"Why are you toying with my honor, Colonel?" Alili pounced on him with the question.

"'Toying with your honor'?! What are you saying?" The Colonel was incredulous.

"Meryouma is still my wife, even though we're divorced."

"That's a new law I hadn't heard of before, Alili."

"Despite the divorce, people still call her Madame Alili. How do you explain that?"

"I have no explanation. What I do know is that she's not under your protection, and that's enough, and then some. We need to find a solution to this problem."

"There's only one answer, sir. Either you marry her according to the custom of God and His Prophet, and she becomes Madame Soltani, or…"

"Or what?"

"Or stay away from her."

"It seems that you would like a war, Alili."

"War? Against whom, sir?"

"Me!"

Soltani got up angrily from his seat, realizing that he had entered into an open confrontation with Alili and needed to be ready to win. After Alili fled the country because of his debts, Soltani and his lover could relax a bit, but they knew it was a temporary respite. The Colonel guessed that Alili's profiteering from cocaine was a quick fix to settle his debts, which would allow him to return home to his country. And then, he would be up to his old tricks again.

Soltani arrived at the office and found his aide Ziane waiting for him. He looked very cheerful.

"Give me what you've got."

"There's a lot of good stuff. Where should I begin?"

"With Nabil Talbi. Who is this fucker?"

"He's Driss Talbi's son."

"I thought the name rang a bell."

"He's also Dolores and Youssef Misbah's nephew, sir."

"Now we understand the secret of his star's rapid rise in the media universe."

Captain Ziane gave a brief report on Nabil Talbi. In 1976, his mother died under mysterious circumstances. It was said that she killed herself by drowning. Nabil was very close to Hoopoe. He was able to use Hoopoe's network of connections to establish a media empire—a newspaper and a television channel primarily. In recent years, the relationship between Nabil Talbi and his uncle, Youssef Misbah, solidified, and the two of them began planning to take over after Hoopoe's long life was over. Their common enemy was Badrou Bouzar; they were afraid he would inherit, as Hoopoe's brother-in-law put it, "the camel and everything it was carrying."

"And what about the veteran guerrilla fighter, Youssef Misbah?"

"His role during the Revolution is truly praiseworthy, but after independence, he threw himself into the embrace of Military Security, sir."

Soltani became increasingly tense as Captain Ziane went into the details of Youssef Misbah's work in Military Security. This apparatus was used as a sword on the necks of members of the military to watch over and terrorize them, just as it was wielded against the general public. President Boumediene was afraid of military coups, especially after the thwarted attempt by Colonel Tahar Zbiri in December 1967, and he gave Military Security and his officers free rein. Rather than defend the interests of the country, they became a tool for repressing citizens, military and civilian alike, exploiting their slip-ups and extorting money from them. A captain in Military Security was much more powerful and feared than someone of higher rank in any other branch of the military.

Ziane mentioned that the former Captain Youssef Misbah officially left Military Security in the late '90s. Still, for all intents and purposes, he remained in that world, making use of his connections, information, and secret files, reaching his hand into the Port of Oran thanks to Hoopoe's influence. He established an import–export company that, in reality, neither imported nor exported a thing. It was a cover for brokering deals and taking commissions from actual merchants and importers in exchange for facilitating customs and administrative matters. A large share of the bribes in hard currency went to his secret accounts in Switzerland and other tax havens. Youssef was considered one of Hoopoe's most important confidants. He knew all his secrets. When oil prices rose in the early aughts, Oran, like other Algerian cities, saw its construction sector flourish. In partnership with Hoopoe and Badrou, Youssef created a large company that secured numerous state-funded projects.

"The construction sector is the best way to launder money," remarked Soltani.

"In our country, financial transactions such as buying and selling are done far from the eyes of banks. No trace of checks, sir."

"Long live *shekara*!"

Soltani smiled as he pronounced the word *shekara*, which, in Algerian, means the plastic sack you wrap large sums of cash in. When he bought his used car four years ago, he remembered being compelled to adhere to the *shekara* system, carrying a black plastic sack with a million centimes in it and handing it over to the seller, who absolutely refused to take a bank check.

Soltani praised his aide's good work and encouraged him to focus and keep going. When Ziane left, he lay back on the large sofa and closed his eyes to relax, but no sooner had he done that than General Belkacemi burst into Soltani's office without knocking. Soltani said to himself: "Come right in." The Boss was not alone. He had brought a guest with him. Soltani got up, clearly annoyed.

"We are honored to be visited by the greatest journalist in the country."

"The honor is mine, Boss."

"You are always welcome, Mr. Nabil."

"May God multiply those like you, Boss."

"May God bless you, Nabil."

Soltani followed this obsequious back-and-forth in silence. What could he say? In these sorts of situations, it was best not to say anything at all.

Nabil reached out to shake the colonel's hand, but he did not meet him halfway. Soltani waited until Nabil's hand had extended all the way to him before lifting his own. After a very quick touch, he withdrew it. He did it out of respect for the presence of his superior, nothing else. After their old dispute surrounding the leak of sensitive information, Nabil tried to appease him in many ways but always found that the door was locked. He waited for the chance to smooth things over, and here it was.

Soltani looked at the Boss disapprovingly and wondered whether this was an appropriate day for visits laden with flowery exchanges. Could he politely excuse himself and say he didn't have time? The Boss understood what was going through his mind, so he put an end to the ambiguity by saying,

"Nabil has come to help us."

"Help us?! Oh, thank God," commented the Colonel in a tone dripping with sarcasm.

"I'm at your service," said Nabil, smiling.

"How?" asked the Colonel.

"He has important information," said the Boss.

"I don't understand," said the Colonel, about to lose his cool.

The Boss told him that Nabil Talbi had some details about Hoopoe's and Badrou Bouzar's murders. How did he know? What business did he have in the investigation anyway? The Boss passed over these points respectfully without presenting any convincing clarification. The Colonel almost lost his mind and screamed in General Belkacemi's face: "This fucker, Nabil Talbi…where does he live? In Algeria? Or Germany or Sweden? Can any journalist in Algeria, no matter his importance, ability, and talent for bootlicking, publish what he wants without getting the green light from his masters?!" He managed to catch hold of himself and remain silent. Best not to light a fire that would be difficult to put out. He looked into Nabil Talbi's eyes as he asked, "What do you have?"

"I have information."

"I'm listening."

"As I said to the Boss, you scratch my back, and I'll scratch yours."

"What do you mean?"

The Boss jumped in and informed the Colonel that he had come to an agreement with Nabil Talbi. He would provide them with any information he had in exchange for journalistic exclusivity. The Colonel was not against the agreement. What mattered to him was solving Hoopoe's and Badrou Bouzar's murders, both on the same day. And what a day! Independence Day was not a pleasant one this year. Hopefully, he would make up for it next year.

The General asked him to sit with Nabil and listen. The Colonel figured he would need the patience of Job to bear sitting with such a person. Possessing a bit of diplomacy was helpful in situations such as these, but the problem was that he was not too good at acting. When he had no respect for someone, he had no interest in dealing with them at all, even if it could be helpful.

Nabil Talbi did not wait for the arrival of the coffee the Boss had ordered to start talking. He spoke like a professional actor who had memorized the scene by heart. He confirmed that Hoopoe and Badrou Bouzar were among the most corrupt men in the country. Not only did he level accusations, but he cited some examples of corrupt operations they were involved in, particularly real estate. Of course, he did not forget to mention that he had unimpeachable documentation he could hand over to investigators and the judiciary at any time. The Colonel did not want to trouble him with such simple and reasonable questions as why he hadn't performed his journalistic duty of informing the public about corruption before today. Why had he decided to reveal them now? And would he publish some of it, or would he use it as leverage? Hoopoe and Badrou were not alone in the world of corruption. They had partners, and he could blackmail them.

The Colonel listened to Nabil Talbi for a while before feeling the need to stop him.

"I'm not concerned with corruption."

"But that's the key, Colonel."

"I want to know who killed Hoopoe and Badrou Bouzar. Do you have an answer or not?"

"I do, Colonel."

"Please speak. My time is limited."

"The killers came from Libya."

"And the proof?"

"You mean the source?"

"Yes."

"The source is a professional secret."

"We're back where we started."

Nabil confirmed that he had irrefutable proof of a scam perpetrated by Hoopoe and Badrou that had cost a terrorist group in Libya dearly. They had sold faulty weapons and received payment in cash. The Libyans exacted revenge on them so their enemies would not laugh at them. They had a highly trained terrorist undertake the operation. He was able to kill and make an example of Miloud's corpse and kill Badrou Bouzar with poison. Here, the Colonel stopped him.

"How did you know Badrou was poisoned?"

"These are professional secrets," smiled Nabil Talbi.

The Colonel likened the journalist to a poker player. He had good cards and was just waiting for the opportunity to double his winnings. He did not provide a single name, a tangible event, or a single piece of verifiable evidence.

After Nabil Talbi left his office, the Colonel called Captain Ziane and asked him to come right away. The aide arrived quickly, and Soltani brought him up to speed on what he had discussed with Nabil Talbi. He believed that individuals like Talbi were simply following orders and held no significance on the chessboard; they were merely pawns that could be moved around and might be sacrificed at any moment when necessary. The problem was that some pawns were deluded and full of swagger. They believe they hold sway and can overturn the balance of power.

"Do you know the source of his information?"

"It might have been the Dove, sir."

Captain Ziane informed him that the Dove was the anonymous source who had provided Nabil Talbi with information. Their correspondence began two months ago with a significant revelation.

"You've piqued my interest."

"Nabil Talbi isn't Driss Talbi's son, sir."

"Who's his father, then?"

"Miloud Sabri."

"Are you sure?"

"The proof is in the documents, sir."

Ziane revealed that the Dove had attached this piece of information to an email document that included a DNA paternity test. Two weeks after receiving it, Nabil contacted his source at the same email, saying he was convinced of the information's veracity. He then thanked him and offered an attractive reward.

16

Spring, Summer, and Fall 1998

The cartoonist Rachid Kadri walked quickly past the Zabana Museum and hailed a taxi. He sat in the back seat and was welcomed by Rabah Driassa's voice on the radio:

Long live my country's sons, and long live its daughters.
There's no need for the envious.

We are the children of Algeria, brothers in all
countries.
My country's sons are brothers that enmity will not
divide, and guns will not lead astray.
They sacrificed for Algeria, answering its call with
jihad.

Long live my country's sons, and long live its daughters.
There's no need for the envious.

Rachid was in a bad mood and almost asked the driver to turn the radio off. He didn't, though. The driver might have been a fan of Driassa and his fervent nationalist songs, so it might have caused a problem. He promised himself he would take revenge on the song with a caricature the next chance he got. News of terrorist massacres was on all the front pages and television broadcasts. The conflict between President Liamine Zéroual and influential generals was at its most intense. People were confused by the fierce media campaign directed at General Mohamed Betchine, the President's political advisor. The country was truly in the eye of the storm, and no one knew what the future held. Rachid had gotten so used to death threats that death had come to feel familiar. Like his fellow journalists, he took precautions. However, he would often say with a tone of resignation, "Who can outrun murder?! They assassinated President Boudiaf six years ago on live television with one of his own bodyguards."

Rachid Kadri started working at an independent newspaper quite by accident in 1990 when one of his journalist friends snatched a bold caricature of President Chadli Bendjedid that Rachid had drawn and gave it to his boss, who asked to meet with the artist. The boss offered him a job at the newspaper, and he accepted. Rachid lambasted absolutely everyone, and no one was spared—the authorities, the Liberation Front Party, the opposition, the Islamists, the communists, and the secularists. He would often quote jokes told by the people of Mascara that he heard during hours he spent in cafés talking with people.

He would then go to his office at the newspaper with the idea for a drawing already in his head. When the drawing was especially bold, he would submit it at the last moment so they wouldn't have a chance to ask him to change it or make it "more polite."

Over ten years, Rachid Kadri and Souad Sabri only fell more in love. He was sure he could not stay away from her. He was like a fish, and Souad was the water, air, life, love, hope, and everything else.

Rachid got out at Khemisti Park and found his beloved Souad waiting for him, but he was not met by her normally cheerful face. He tried to get her to smile with a new joke about people from Mascara, but she remained as silent and unmovable as a stone. She did not want to say anything, so he took matters into his own hands.

"What is it, Souad?"

"Terrible news... I'm pregnant."

"Are you sure?"

"Yes."

Tears ran down her cheeks. He took her hand and had her look into his eyes as he told her he was crazy about her and could not live without her. He reassured her and promised they would find a solution.

"Where's the solution, Rachid?"

"We need a doctor."

"It's late. I'm in my third month."

"Why did you hide this from me, Souad?"

"I thought I could solve the problem myself."

Souad was terrified. If her father found out about the pregnancy, he would make their lives a living hell. He would not allow his reputation to be sullied. Hoopoe had been telling his wife that he had been patient with Souad, hoping she would return to the right path and understand what was best for her. He had not yet accepted the failure of his plan to marry her to the General's son, and he could not keep Rachid away from her despite many attempts to do so.

Souad's life with Rachid was an adventure within yet more adventures. Thanks to him, she had a renewed love for life and had stopped taking sedatives. One day, Souad said to her mother, "Rachid is the doctor, and love is the cure."

But despite the close relationship she had with her mother, she could not tell her about the pregnancy. She felt so ashamed and feared her reaction. If her mother found out, she might never forgive her.

Rachid and Souad appealed to Falcon for help. They went to see him in his office in Sidi Houari. Falcon listened to the details and could not hide how troubled he was by the news. He remained silent without commenting. Then, he asked them to wait in the reception room while he made a phone call, hoping to find a way out. They waited, knowing Falcon was their last resort. If he did not help them quickly, they were sunk.

Falcon called Stork and told him everything. They both agreed that Hoopoe would not stand idly by. They needed to find a solution right away. They considered multiple scenarios but couldn't decide on one. After much back and forth, Stork said, "There is one solution."

"What's that?"

"They come stay with me."

"Wouldn't that be a lot for you?"

"Quite the contrary. Everything about Souad reminds me of Dolores."

Rachid and Souad arrived in Tamanrasset after traveling for two days and over two thousand kilometers by land. They refused to fly to avoid leaving any traces behind them. Stork sent a trusted friend to Oran to bring them safely in his car.

The months of the pregnancy passed quickly. Souad gave birth at home, not in the hospital, and when Rachid and Souad asked Stork to name the new baby, he immediately came up with "Zuhour."

Of course, he did not say why, but when Falcon learned about it, he smiled and understood that Stork's heart had decided; he remembered that Stork used to call his beloved Zahra by that name. They all agreed to register Zuhour officially as Stork's daughter out of fear of Hoopoe's wrath.

Two months after Zuhour was born, Souad read in one of the national newspapers that her mother had been in a terrible traffic accident and that her life was in danger. She insisted on returning to Oran to make sure her mother was okay. Stork, Falcon, and Rachid tried to persuade her to reconsider, but it was futile. Rachid would not permit her to travel alone, so he accompanied her. Thus, they returned to Oran by land and left baby Zuhour in Tamanrasset in the care of Stork and his family. They avoided hotels and stayed in the apartment of Rachid's journalist friend, Mehdi, who had fled to Paris because of terrorist threats to journalists. As soon as they arrived, Souad began gathering information about her mother and planning to visit her, all while keeping it a secret from her father.

In the meantime, Hoopoe learned from Badrou Bouzar about his childhood friend, Redouane Derbal, who had run away and gotten involved in numerous terrorist operations.

"I know where he is and can lead the security forces to him so they can arrest him and his group," boasted Badrou.

"Maybe a better solution can be found."

"What do you mean, Uncle Miloud?"

"Redouane is a sheep. Maybe we can find a use for him."

Indeed, Hoopoe began experimenting by assigning some missions to Redouane to liquidate opponents who were of no more use to him. There was a bank manager who stood in the way of a loan he needed to seal an important deal; he was killed on his way home from work. No investigation or anything of the sort. Badrou was the go-between who passed along the orders. He convinced Redouane that he was active in an Islamist cell within the army, which filled him with enthusiasm. Redouane became a mercenary without knowing it. The most important operation he was given was to kill Souad and Rachid. After their sudden disappearance, Hoopoe looked for them everywhere. He quickly deduced that they had run off together. But where? Had they fled abroad? Souad's passport was in his possession, and he was sure they had not left the country through transit points in airports, ports, or crossing areas along the borders. Finally, Hoopoe got the information he was looking for. He learned the truth after questioning her friend Aïcha.

"Souad is pregnant by Rachid."

Hoopoe resisted telling his wife, Dolores, and his brother-in-law, Youssef, about this catastrophe. He resolved to get rid of them right away. As long as they remained alive, it threatened everything he had built. After eight months of searching, he was about to give up. He could not find any trace of them. Then, he devised a scheme that ended up paying off. He bided his time until Dolores traveled to France to undergo some medical tests and leaked a false piece of news to the press that she had been in a terrible traffic accident and that her life was hanging by a thread. Three days later, Souad and her lover had fallen into the trap. Hoopoe swore he would show them no mercy.

Badrou Bouzar knew Souad and Rachid had run off, but he was unaware of the pregnancy. When Hoopoe asked Badrou to put his friend, Redouane, in charge of getting rid of them, Badrou understood that the motive was to avenge his tarnished honor. Redouane completed half the mission. He killed Souad but only lightly wounded Rachid. When Redouane realized that the target of the operation was Hoopoe's daughter, he pressed Badrou for the truth. Then he threatened him. Badrou had no choice but to reveal what he had been hiding. Redouane insisted on meeting Hoopoe personally. Miloud was furious with Badrou for disclosing his identity, knowing that Redouane would likely try to blackmail him. He decided that the time had come to slaughter the Eid sheep *and* teach Badrou a lesson he would never forget.

"You need to prove to me that you can be trusted."

"What do you want me to do, Uncle Miloud?"

"Kill Redouane like the sheep he is."

"I've never killed anyone in my life."

"Killing is a trade you can learn anytime."

What could Badrou do? Could he disobey him? Hoopoe accompanied Badrou to a house where Redouane was hiding in Sidi El Bachir, and they found him waiting. Hoopoe took out his favorite dagger and stabbed Redouane in the stomach. He fell. Then, he ordered Badrou to finish the operation. At first, he was frightened, his hand trembling. Then he plucked up his courage and took the dagger from Hoopoe. He leaned over Redouane and fell on him with several stabs until he was a lifeless corpse.

Hoopoe took the dagger and put it in his bag. After making sure no one saw them, they left the apartment.

The next day, while Badrou was sipping coffee in Hoopoe's office, Hoopoe looked at him seriously and said, "I have decided to hold on to the dagger that was used to kill Redouane."

"This dagger is dangerous for us, Uncle Miloud."

"Dangerous for *you*! I'll be fine."

It was then that Badrou remembered that Hoopoe was wearing gloves when he had stabbed Redouane. There was silence for a moment. Then Hoopoe approached Badrou and whispered in his ear: "I'll never use this dagger again, and your fingerprints will always be on it. Do you understand now?"

"I understand, Uncle Miloud."

Hoopoe explained his philosophy of partnership to him. He told him that a good partnership always needed guarantees against betrayal. Then he reassured him, "Our fates are intertwined because we're in the same boat, brother."

Badrou Bouzar understood the message and realized that his life was in Hoopoe's hands.

Two months after Souad's murder, Rachid Kadri decided to join his friend, Mehdi, in Paris. He was convinced that he had to leave the country immediately. There was no hope in remaining. He got a French visa with the help of his boss at the newspaper. The night before he was to travel, he drank heavily and cried to the melodies of Cheb Hasni, who had been assassinated when he was twenty-six years old.

I've left her in your care
Take care of her; don't harm her
She's my beloved
It wasn't meant to be.

Rachid broke into sobs. For his beloved Souad, whose love he had not had enough of yet. For his newborn daughter, Zuhour, whom he left behind. He cried for himself, his youth, and the Algeria they had sullied and made into a joke.

Rachid arrived in Paris in the evening. He put off calling his friend, Mehdi, because he wanted to spend some time alone in the City of Lights. He spent hours wandering its narrow streets, feeling some affection for the area around Saint-Michel. He ate dinner at a small restaurant that specialized in French dishes, ordering cheese fondue and drinking expensive aged wine. He thought about celebrating something but couldn't quite figure out what. Was this a new beginning? Was this a celebration for being rescued from hell? Could there be a heaven without Souad? He couldn't think straight, and after drinking quite a bit, he headed for a hotel on Rue Jacob, where he fell asleep in his clothes. He didn't usually sleep so well in a new bed, especially on the first night, but that night, he slept peacefully and without nightmares.

The next day, he called Mehdi and found him at the peak of anxiety. Mehdi thought he had not been able to leave the country. He had thought the worst, imagining they had finally done away with him. Mehdi told him that he had called common friends in Oran numerous times. They all said he had disappeared. Mehdi thought he had been kidnapped, tortured, and had his head cut off. He was waiting for news of his murder. And when Rachid told him the truth, he was furious and proceeded to curse him in every language he knew. Rachid let him be until he had worn himself out.

Rachid found his friend in good health, living with a French journalist named Katherine. He had started to smoke Camels instead of Nassims. He didn't ask about Algeria because he read about it daily and knew what was going on there from his work as a journalist. He was happy to be living in France and told him about his future projects, which were far from Algeria. Then he suggested that

Rachid work with tourists as a caricature artist. He could earn good money.

"There's nothing good in Algeria, Rachid."

"Algeria is us. You and me," he said as he lit a Nassim.

Mehdi got up angrily and yelled, "God damn Nassims and everything they represent!"

Rachid spent two weeks in Paris. For the first few days, things were fine, but it was not long before he started to struggle with sleep and was seized with anxiety. He realized that the only way out was to go back to Oran. Mehdi tried to convince him in every way he could think of to reconsider, but he was unable to. He went with Rachid to Charles de Gaulle Airport and cried when he said goodbye, as if he were accompanying him to his final resting place.

Early elections followed President Liamine Zéroual's resignation announcement. Hoopoe suggested to Nabil that he profit from his studies in media and establish a newspaper. Hoopoe, of course, would take care of the details, such as securing administrative approval, financing, and publicity. Nabil was convinced that Badrou was conspiring against him and wanted to get rid of him. Badrou thought the same thing. It was clear to anyone watching that Hoopoe was deviously using them both. They would lash out at one another while Hoopoe watched and laughed. Nabil had to put up with everything to achieve his goal. Thus, he decided to play a strong card to get closer to his Uncle Hoopoe and neutralize the threat of

Badrou Bouzar. He asked for the hand of Hoopoe's daughter, Mona, who had become a widow following her first husband's death. Hoopoe's face darkened with anger. Nabil thought he would be happy and embrace him.

"Why, Uncle Miloud? I come to you with all good intentions."

"Mona is your sister."

"My sister?!"

"I mean, she's like your sister. And besides, marriage might ruin our relationship. Forget about it, understand?"

"I understand, Uncle Miloud."

That evening, Hoopoe offered to marry his older daughter, Mona, to Badrou, who accepted. Mona was not as pretty as her sister, Souad, or her mother. And she had not inherited a tenth of Hoopoe's intelligence. She was crude, arrogant, and could not bear children. Of course, Badrou knew all of that but decided to risk it anyway. He realized that the necessary price was steep; he would be denied the opportunity of becoming a father, but he was convinced that becoming Hoopoe's son-in-law would open up all manner of opportunities for him.

Souad's killing was a horrible blow to Dolores. If not for her faith in God and fate, she would have gone crazy. She knew that her nephew, Nabil, had asked for Mona's hand and that her husband had refused.

"Why?"

"I have my reasons."

"And they are?"

"Marriage among relatives causes diseases."

Dolores's suspicions and concerns began to sharpen when he asked her to swear to stop any plans that involved Mona and Nabil. Then, he insisted on marrying Mona to his aide, Badrou Bouzar. Dolores was not happy, but she couldn't stop the plan because Mona had agreed to it.

Dolores decided to investigate the matter on her own, in complete secrecy. She returned to when Driss Talbi, or Falcon, was in prison between 1965 and 1967. At that time, rumors circulated that there was a sexual relationship between her husband and her sister, Farida. She had quickly put the idea out of her mind, but now, the question weighed heavily on her: What if Nabil was Hoopoe's son?

She thought about it for a while and arrived at a definitive plan for confirming the issue of paternity.

She took samples of Hoopoe's and Nabil's hair and asked a police officer friend to run a DNA test. Of course, she lied to him about the reasons. She told him it had to do with a father searching for his lost son who had come to her charitable organization that provides aid to orphans. After a few weeks, she received the results: Hoopoe was Nabil Talbi's father.

After thinking about it long and hard, she decided not to confront her husband with the truth and to hide the secret to prevent the destruction of what was left of her family, and to protect Falcon's reputation.

Amira Derbal went with her mother to Badrou Bouzar's office, where they were warmly welcomed. Badrou had stopped wearing the long white robe in favor of a suit and tie. Her mother asked for some help related to navigating the public hospital system to deal with some health problems she was having, and Badrou promised he would use his influence and take care of things as soon as possible. When they got up to go, Badrou gave her mother a sum of money. He then looked at the little girl and asked her, "How old are you, Amira?"

"Eight, Uncle Badrou."

"God bless. What do you want to be when you grow up?"

"A policewoman."

"Why?"

"To put evildoers behind bars."

Badrou laughed and gave her a kiss on the right cheek. He disgusted her, and she wanted to squeeze his neck so hard he would die.

Driss Talbi visited Professeur Rondeau at the retirement home in Gambetta, as he did occasionally. They sat in the garden, surrounded by sadness. Algeria was going from bad to worse, and there was no way out on the horizon. Algerians of European and foreign descent had become the preferred targets for terrorists. The teacher was forced to give up his home in Plateau Saint-Michel following the assassination of Bishop Pierre Claverie on August 1, 1996, at his residence in Oran's Saint-Eugène Church. He had found safety in this home run by the

Catholic Little Sisters of the Poor, where he could spend his final years.

"Cain has won again, Professeur."

"Yes. Algeria has become Cain's paradise," he said, fighting back tears.

Driss gently pulled him close and hugged him.

17

Thursday, July 5, 2018

9:05 P.M.

Colonel Karim Soltani returned to Sidi Houari. He drove around the neighborhood between buildings and streets that all looked the same before finally finding his way to the right place. There were almost no lights, and he only found the building after some effort. He went up the stairs and stood in front of the apartment on the second floor. He rang the bell three times. Falcon, wearing pajamas, opened the door for him. He looked surprised. Soltani understood by the way Falcon was looking at him that he was not welcome. Nevertheless, Falcon invited him in and went with him to his office. Then he signaled for him to sit in the chair in front of him.

"Pardon me, Mr. Talbi. I know it's late."

"What is it?"

"I want to confirm an important piece of information."

"About what, sir?"

"Your son."

"Nabil?"

"He's your son?"

"I don't understand."

"Is he your son or not?"

"Are you drunk, sir?!"

"Nabil is Hoopoe's son. I have proof."

Falcon quickly regained his composure. He got up from his chair, walked over to the window, and opened it. He took a deep breath, then looked at him, saying, "You said you have proof."

"That's right."

The Colonel took a copy of the DNA report from his pocket and handed it to him. Falcon put his glasses on and glanced at it. He realized that he could no longer hide the truth. He bowed his head and proceeded to tell him how, after his second marriage, he had discovered that he could not have children as a result of the torture he had been subjected to during two separate periods. The first was at the hands of the French, and the second with the Algerians. Then he talked about his former wife, Farida, and the role she played in betraying Yazid, their direct superior in the Revolution. He spoke about how Abbas Badi also became a victim of this betrayal, for which he paid a heavy price. Falcon lifted the veil on many details surrounding the death, or rather, the murder of his wife, Farida, and the slaughter of the freedom fighter, Cherif Miqdad. He mentioned that he had called Hoopoe and told him about Cherif's confession and accusation against Farida.

"Was Hoopoe the only one who knew about it, sir?"

"Yes, he was."

"Meaning he's the one who killed Cherif Miqdad and Farida?"

"I'm sure of it."

"There's one question that baffles me, sir."

"What's that, Colonel?"

"Why didn't you suspect Hoopoe?"

"Hoopoe was practically my brother. It never occurred to me that he would betray me."

"And have you spoken with Nabil about this?"

"No . . . I can't."

"Why not?"

"I'm scared for him."

Falcon got up from his chair, and a single tear fell from his eye. He looked at Soltani and said, "The truth is a sickness, sir."

"There's no use running from sickness though."

"Would you like to know the truth, Colonel?"

"The truth is all an investigator wants."

"Isn't a confession the best of all proofs?"

"It is. You know the law."

"I'm the one who killed Hoopoe."

"All by yourself?"

"Yes, sir."

He followed protocol and told Falcon that he was under arrest.

Soltani returned to his office on Rue Larribère and brought his aides, Derraji and Ziane, up to speed on the latest. He lingered on Falcon's confession. There were real motives for taking revenge on Hoopoe, but Falcon was not the killer, or at least not the only killer. So, who was his accomplice then? When he finished, Derraji took a piece of paper out of her pocket and put it in front of her, saying, "We have the proof, sir... Zuhour Badi is Stork's daughter."

"And she denied it to...?" asked Soltani.

"To buy time," answered Ziane.

"And to throw us off Stork's trail," added Derraji.

Soltani quickly glanced at Zuhour's birth certificate. She was born in Tamanrasset in 1998. The father was listed as Abbas Badi, and the mother was Safia Agh Hassani.

"We need to know if Abbas Badi is still alive," said the Colonel.

"There's no trace of him in the death register," Derraji replied.

He lost himself in thought for more than a minute as he tried to tie together different pieces of information. Then he looked at his aides and said, "Zuhour isn't Stork's daughter."

"What do you mean, sir?" asked Derraji.

"I think Zuhour is the daughter of Rachid Kadri and Souad Sabri," he said, with a look of self-satisfaction.

Soltani put a bunch of printed pictures he had taken during his tour of Rachid's apartment down on the desk and shuffled through them. Zuhour resembled Souad for sure, and there was a photo of Souad holding an infant with her beloved next to her. Zuhour had keys to Rachid Kadri's apartment and could come and go as she pleased. She did not show any of the usual signs of shyness or shame when she found herself in front of the Colonel in the home of a man she was supposedly not linked to by birth.

Fifteen minutes later, he was just about done eating a chicken sandwich when he received a call from the Boss. General Belkacemi informed him that an important guest would visit him shortly, then hung up. He did not mention the guest's name, but the suspense lasted only for a few moments. Soltani heard a knock on the door and saw Youssef Misbah enter with a smile on his face. He indicated for him to sit down. Youssef thanked him.

"I'd like to know where the investigation stands right now, sir," said Youssef.

"We have theories and are looking for proof."

"Any news on the Libyans, Colonel?"

"The Libyans have nothing to do with it."

"I worry the case will drag on for too long and go off course."

"It's the first day, Mr. Misbah!"

The Colonel was not comfortable with this visit or with this discussion. Youssef Misbah was a graduate of the Military Security School. He embodied the cunning traits of a fox, wolf, and viper. He carefully weighed every word before speaking. The Colonel was almost certain the reason for the visit was not to see where the investigation stood; there was definitely another goal. He remained as patient as possible after such a hard day, letting the retired captain reveal his cards. The room was quiet, but Youssef quickly stepped forward to break the silence.

"I'm one of you. I sacrificed my youth in the army."

"Thank you for your service."

"I came to you about a sensitive matter, sir."

"I'm all ears."

Youssef Misbah prefaced his words by saying that he was not speaking for himself but rather that he represented his family, specifically the two widows, his sister, Zahra, and her daughter, Mona. The killing of Miloud Sabri and Badrou Bouzar on the same day was a massive blow to the family. It would be even bigger if the details were to get out. The shame of the scandal would be devastating. Slitting the throat and then cutting the nose off are not trivial matters. The priority was to close the case as soon as possible. The longer it took, the more dangerous it would get, and the fire would spread. The fire needed to be put out without delay. And if there wasn't sufficient proof to accuse the Libyans, it was wrong to pin the crime on Algerians.

"What will our enemies say, Colonel? Algerians killing Algerians on this blessed Independence Day! This is a disgrace to Algeria as much as it is a disgrace to Miloud Sabri's family."

The Colonel listened to Misbah's plea without interrupting him. When he was finished, Soltani turned to him and asked, "What do you want, Mr. Misbah?"

"To nip the scandal in the bud."

"Nip the truth in the bud?!"

"The *scandal*, not the truth."

"Ah, the scandal. I get it. And the truth, Mr. Misbah?"

"'The living outlast the dead,' as they say in Egypt."

"And justice?"

"God's justice is better than man's justice. Thank God for the blessing of Islam."

"God guides that which He has created. Thank you for your visit, Mr. Misbah."

He got up from his chair, and there was rage in Youssef Misbah's eyes as he left the office.

Soltani was lost in thought when First Lieutenant Derraji rushed in. She came around his desk and stood beside him, holding her cell phone screen in front of him. She showed him a video taken from a camera located on the street where the Mistress's Villa was. The recording went back to the night before Miloud Sabri's murder. It showed Rachid Kadri running.

Soltani decided to move fast and confront Rachid Kadri with the video. Would he also consider his presence close to the crime scene a coincidence? He was not convinced of Rachid's explanation of the drawing of Brother Bandit without a nose. The video was a new and vital piece of evidence against him.

Soltani headed to Rachid Kadri's apartment in November 1st Square and rang the bell. The beautiful young woman he had seen before opened the door for him. He spoke first.

"Hello, Miss Zuhour Badi, or should I say, Miss Kadri?"

"What do you want with us?" she responded angrily.

"I want the truth, miss."

Rachid Kadri was quietly following the conversation when Soltani turned to him.

"You're the one who killed Hoopoe, Mr. Kadri."

"That's right."

"Who was your accomplice?"

"I always work alone."

"You're a liar, Mr. Kadri."

Soltani brought up the surveillance camera footage that implicated Rachid, as well as the drawing of Brother Bandit without a nose. Right then, a person entered the living room.

"I'm the one who killed Hoopoe."

"Who are you?"

"I am Abbas Badi."

Soltani saw a man dressed in Tuareg clothing walking toward him.

"Who was your accomplice?"

"I killed him myself," answered Stork.

"That's not true. There's someone else," said Soltani.

"Me," said Rachid.

"No, it's me," said Zuhour.

He gazed at them in astonishment. It was the first time he had witnessed a competition to confess to a murder. Right then, his cell phone rang. He answered it without looking at the caller's number.

"I have new information on the cocaine case, sir."

"For crying out loud. What now?!"

Ziane plunged into the details, revealing that Tariq, General Belkacemi's son, belonged to a ring of sons of high-ranking officials in the army, customs, security, state organizations, and the business world.

"Where is Tariq now?"

"He left Oran Airport three hours ago for Barcelona, sir."

"And he'll come back when things have calmed down, right?"

"That's the scenario, sir."

Soltani ended the call feeling a degree of pessimism as he thought about the children of leaders. Algerians would need a miracle to see these corrupt people behind bars. His cell phone rang again. He glanced at the number and saw it was General Belkacemi.

"We have another murder, Soltani."

"Who's the victim this time, sir?"

"Youssef Misbah."

"Was his throat slit or was he poisoned?

"Strangled. Luckily, we have the killer this time."

"Who is it, sir?"

"Go to the Hotel Royale right now, and you'll know everything soon enough."

18

Winter and Spring 2011

Badrou Bouzar met Amira Derbal again quite by accident at a relative's wedding in Sidi El Bachir. She was with her sick mother. Badrou could not believe his eyes that the little girl he had last seen years before had grown into such a beautiful young woman; this child who had told him she wanted to be a policewoman, arresting evildoers when she grew up. Amira's family always mentioned how much Badrou did for them. He had attended Redouane's funeral in defiance of the security apparatuses, but, in fact, everything was prepared like a play, and he acted his assigned role as well as could be expected. The authorities did not release the bodies of terrorists, forcing their families to be satisfied with condolences, under surveillance, of course. Badrou arrived at the house of his childhood friend, Redouane, in Sidi El Bachir, sobbing over the loss. It was easy for him to shed tears; all he had to do was picture his drunken father beating his mother. As soon as he left the mourning household, security personnel arrived in civilian clothing and "arrested" him in front of everyone there. They shoved him into a black car, and he was transformed into a hero in the eyes of the Islamists and terrorists. This made them trust him more and provide him with valuable information. Following this, Badrou related new details about that heroic event to Amira's family, telling them he was tortured for three straight days before they released him. Amira grew up hearing her mother talk about him and all his attributes. She prayed for him and considered him a son. But Badrou's assistance and kindness to them was not an expiation for a sin. Rather, it was to remain a shining star in the Islamists' universe.

Badrou became obsessed with Amira. He thought about her constantly and sought out any opportunity to see her. He dedicated an entire day to her, following her by car from the moment she left home in the morning until she arrived at the law office in Gambetta, where she worked as a secretary. He then went to work but returned just before noon to wait for her again. When she came out, he approached her and stopped his car, pretending their meeting was accidental. After exchanging greetings and pleasantries, he invited her to a nearby cafeteria. At first, she hesitated, but then she agreed.

Marrying Mona Sabri was a blessing and a curse for Badrou. Mona never let the opportunity slip to remind him where he came from; she would deliberately humiliate him in front of everyone. Oh, how he hated her! He used to console himself by saying that the situation would not last forever and that her father, Hoopoe, would leave this world sooner or later. Once that happened, Mona would receive what she deserved, and then some. He swore to God he would wipe the floor with her and make her life a living hell. What he wanted more than anything was a son to carry on his name. He thought about secretly taking on another wife, but rejected the idea, afraid of Hoopoe's reaction when he found out about it. He used to say to himself that there was no way of getting rid of the barren Mona before getting rid of her father, Hoopoe.

Driss Talbi, aka Falcon, was as happy as could be when he heard Tunisian President Ben Ali say at the end of his speech: "I understand you." Three words that summed up everything. Falcon enthusiastically participated in a television program on the Arab Spring and warned of the consequences of imitating the Algerian experience in the '90s by mixing religion, the military, and politics. He guaranteed that using terrorism as a way to scare everyone into complacency was a surefire way to destroy all projects of change.

"Seeking refuge in terrorism is playing with fire."

He pointed to the legacy of terrorism in Algeria: a hundred and fifty to two hundred thousand people killed. Add to that thousands of people missing. As for material losses, they came to twenty billion dollars, a frighteningly high price to pay. Was it possible to wipe away the memory of ruthless, blind killings with the stroke of a pen or a presidential decree? Falcon was never convinced of the prevailing view that the Peace and Reconciliation Law of 2005 would turn the bloody page of the past.

"When was turning the page ever the appropriate solution? Shouldn't we at least read the page before turning it once and for all?"

Hoopoe followed the collapse of the regimes in Tunisia and Egypt live on Al Jazeera. No one expected them to collapse so quickly. How much that slogan made him laugh: "The people . . . want . . . to bring down the regime!" He wondered if power had truly come to be held in the people's hands. Could the flock really drive the shepherd? He thought about the Algerian experience in the '90s. It could be exported to other places. Arabs needed to believe that there were two options, no more: either they take cover in the embrace of the military or fall into the Islamist trap. There was no third option. And he laughed when he read a statement from his former comrade, Falcon, saying that the alternative was to form a democratic front to face the military and the Islamists together. Hoopoe said to his wife, Dolores, "Poor Falcon, still dreaming of an alternative. There's no alternative under the sun. It's either black or white."

Hoopoe was optimistic about the future of the Arab Spring. The lack of stability was an opportunity to shuffle the deck and bet on new players and horses. During discussions with his close aides and partners, such as Youssef Misbah, Badrou Bouzar, and Nabil Talbi, Hoopoe would explain his theory in great detail: Terrorism provided the best environment for human and financial investment. It was not true that investment depended on stability and the establishment of security. The complete opposite was true—profitable investment required instability. Chaos was a plus because it allowed for the release of hidden energies and spurred creativity and initiative. Terrorism was a guaranteed investment, providing great services to many people. It could be used to convince citizens of the necessity to limit their personal freedom in exchange for protection. This is what the White House did in the United States following the attacks of September 11, 2001. Opposition voices could be silenced by accusing them of terrorism or supporting terrorism. Arms dealers could amass fortunes, and on and on.

Hoopoe often cited the Algerian situation. If not for the Terrorist Decade, the '90s, a new class of entrepreneurs and the new rich would not have emerged. The Black Decade, as it had come to be called, was not a curse for all Algerians. Many benefited from it, and it was their right to call it the Golden Decade.

Badrou Bouzar met with Amira Derbal. He placed his hand on hers as they drove around Aïn El Turk in his new car. Then he tried to kiss her, but she pretended to be annoyed and angry. He smiled and explained that his intentions were honorable. He would not extend a forbidden hand to the sister of his dearest friend, Redouane. Badrou became increasingly attached to her, wanting to see her every day, and not in secret, either. He arrived at a reasonable solution. He offered her a job as his secretary.

Amira began working with Badrou, who desired her constant presence. Their relationship evolved into a romantic affair, with Amira becoming his mistress. She said to him more than once, "I'll only live with you lawfully, which means the only solution is for us to get married according to the custom of God and His Prophet."

"That's a declaration of war on Mona and her father."

"I don't see any other solution, Badrou."

"Be patient, Amira. 'And whosoever fears God, He will appoint for him a way out.' God Almighty has spoken the truth."

Amira decided to make the best of this situation and waited for the opportunity to achieve her goal.

Rachid entered a tunnel of depression following the murder of his beloved Souad.

And whenever the sickness worsened, Driss would take him to Abbas in Tamanrasset, where he would spend a few weeks in the desert until he improved. Then he would return to Oran to take up the battle again. He did not wish to abandon his readers. Once, a woman who came looking for him at the newspaper told him, "I wouldn't be able to put up with how awful this country is without your drawings that lift my spirits every morning."

Rachid Kadri received lots of fan mail from people thanking him and encouraging him to continue. To all those who urged him to be careful and avoid conflicts, he said, "Should I betray the people who put their trust in me? Should I deprive them of a little joy? No. Never!"

The desert was, for him, a place to meditate and relax. And when his condition improved, he would turn into a little kid. He would play with Zuhour, who called him "uncle," not knowing he was actually her father. He would say to those close to him who knew his secret, "If not for Zuhour, I would have put an end to this harsh life a long time ago."

Zuhour grew up quickly and resembled her mother, Souad, more and more. She began to ask serious questions and came to understand the truth of her past and present. One time, she found a picture of herself as an infant in her mother's arms as she stood next to Rachid. Zuhour persisted in asking until Abbas was compelled to reveal the whole truth.

Zuhour grew up in Abbas's embrace, and he loved her like his own two daughters and grandchildren. When she was a little girl, she insisted on seeing his face, crying nonstop until she got her way. He sat her in front of him and removed the gauze. The little girl's reaction was not what he expected. Rather than continuing to cry or being scared by the sight of a man without a nose, she exploded into laughter. As time went on, his confidence in Zuhour began to grow. He began to reveal secrets to her one by one. He told her the story of his love for her grandmother, Dolores, and how her grandfather had betrayed him. He swore to her that he would avenge his honor no matter how long it took.

Nabil devoted a great deal of time and effort to strengthening his position. He never trusted Badrou. He knew Hoopoe would side with his daughter's husband if he were forced to choose between them. Therefore, he set out to deepen the relationship with his Uncle Youssef. He thought the time had come to take the pulse of the situation and consider who would succeed Hoopoe, who was approaching eighty.

"God bless you, Uncle Youssef."

"May God bless you with confidence, Nabil."

"We have one problem."

"I know... the Islamist Badrou Bouzar."

"We need to eat him for lunch before he eats us for dinner, Uncle."

"Exactly."

Youssef Misbah warned Nabil that Badrou was dangerous and changed colors like a chameleon. He no doubt had a plan to inherit Hoopoe's fortune. Youssef had some suggestions, including spying on him through people around him. He told Nabil that Badrou had fallen in love with a beautiful young woman who had started to work as his secretary. They might get her to work with them.

Amira Derbal received a phone call from Youssef Misbah. He wanted to see her urgently and requested that she keep it a secret from Badrou. They arranged to meet at the Hotel Royale that evening. When she arrived, she found him sipping a beer at the bar. He dove into an extensive review of her background and history, knowing practically everything about her. Badrou had told her about Youssef and his prior work in the intelligence service, so she was not surprised.

"What do you want, Monsieur Misbah?"

"Work with us, Amira."

"Who are you?"

“We’re Hoopoe’s heirs who have come to finally claim what’s ours.”

“I need to think about it.”

“We don’t have much time. Are you in or not?”

“I’m in.”

Amira thought spying on Badrou for Youssef Misbah was a golden opportunity that could not be wasted. The offer met her expectations and fulfilled her conditions. Youssef’s protection would reduce the risks to her. Amira did not agree to betray Badrou out of a desire for money, though. She agreed in order to take revenge on the two people who killed Redouane, her only brother. She still remembered that day in 1998 when she was eight years old.

Redouane had asked her to stay in one of the rooms of the apartment where he was hiding in the Sidi El Bachir neighborhood before his friend Badrou arrived with another man. It wasn’t long before the two guests arrived. Soon, she heard the rising voices of an argument, so she opened the door a crack to take a look and saw Badrou Bouzar (or Uncle Badrou, as she called him at the time) and a man she didn’t know (Badrou called him “Uncle Miloud”) stabbing Redouane in the stomach. She remained glued to where she was standing, unable to make a sound, she was so shocked. When the two killers left, she approached her brother and saw his eyes bulging wide open, staring at the ceiling, the blood flowing down his sides. She fled the house to seek help from her mother, but then remained silent, concealing the truth about the two murderers. Years passed, but she never forgot. Whenever she recalled that crime scene, she swore she would take revenge sooner or later.

19

Thursday, July 5, 2018

10:09 P.M.

Colonel Karim Soltani arrived at the Hotel Royale, one of the most luxurious hotels in Oran, as night was falling over the city. He found the hotel manager waiting for him at the entrance. The man, a middle-aged, thin, and tall figure, sported a large mustache that hung over his upper lip. He chewed on a cigarette with his front teeth, his eyes darting left and right. Everything looked normal to the Colonel. No trace of police, ambulances, or throngs of journalists and onlookers. He saw that the bar was teeming with well-to-do customers who could afford to enjoy a glass of Ricard, whiskey, or a cold beer, unlike the broke alcohol lovers who could only drink in abandoned houses, forests, or on beaches.

He concluded that the most recent crime had been kept under wraps like the previous two. The manager escorted him to the second floor and knocked on a door, which was opened by a police officer. The manager stepped aside, and the Colonel went in. His eyes fell on the body of Youssef Misbah on the bed. Then he turned to his left and saw a man sitting and smoking, his hands cuffed.

"So, you're the murderer! Did you kill Hoopoe, as well?" asked Soltani.

"Yes, I did."

"Who was your accomplice?"

"No accomplice."

"And the motive?"

"There is none."

"I think the motive is that your true father, Hoopoe, and your uncle, Youssef Misbah, killed Farida, your mother."

Soltani ordered the policeman to leave and wait outside the room as Nabil drew on the cigarette to hide his nervousness. Then, his tongue loosened, and he began to talk. He was at home when his mother received a phone call from Hoopoe on that unfortunate day. They argued. He heard her say she would reveal everything, then rushed out after kissing him on the cheek and leaving him at the neighbor's place. He looked out the window and saw her standing on the sidewalk. Then, a Citroën CX arrived. He was very familiar with that car, having ridden in it many times. At first, his mother refused to get in. His uncle Youssef, who was sitting next to Hoopoe, got out and slapped her, forcing her to go with them. Nabil stopped talking as tears began to run down his cheeks. The Colonel did not want to fill the silence, so he let him catch his breath.

"I didn't do a thing to defend and save my mother, sir."

"You were a child. But why didn't you tell your father...I mean, Driss?"

"Out of fear."

"And the fear turned into a desire for revenge."

"Exactly, sir."

"Here's the scoop you've been looking for, and you'll be one of its heroes, Nabil."

"There won't be any scoop, sir."

"What do you mean? I don't understand."

"You'll know everything soon enough."

"I don't like riddles. Could you be more clear?"

"I won't say another word, sir."

Soltani returned to his office, and his aide, Captain Samir Ziane, told him that he had discovered a copy of Amira Derbal's diary on her personal computer. In it, she describes Badrou Bouzar and Hoopoe in the harshest terms and vows to take revenge on them.

"And did you find a reason for this hatred?" asked Soltani.

"Badrou and Hoopoe killed her brother, Redouane Derbal, the fugitive terrorist, in 1998."

"And so, a piece of the puzzle falls into place, Captain Ziane."

Despite how late it was, the Colonel decided to pay someone an urgent visit. He hoped it would be the last visit of this momentous and blessed day. He drove his car through the streets of Oran, which had surrendered to the night's calm. It did not take long to get to Saint-Eugène. He rang the bell, and Amira Derbal opened the door. She did not have a hijab on, her short blond hair visible, and she was wearing Kabyle clothes. She looked completely different without the hijab. He entered without waiting for permission, walked to the living room, and sat down. Fairouz's voice hung in the air:

I loved you in the summer. I loved you in the winter.
I waited for you in the summer. I waited for you in the winter.
Your eyes are the summer, and my eyes are the winter.
We will meet, my love,
Beyond the summer… and beyond the winter.

Amira caught up to him and turned off the stereo. Then she sat on one side of the room and tried not to show any signs of surprise or unease with this extremely late visit.

"Tell me, Amira. Were you crying for Badrou today or for someone else?"

"I don't understand the question, sir."

"Were you crying for Badrou or Redouane?"

"Redouane?"

"Your brother."

She continued to pretend she did not understand what he meant. The Colonel felt that the charade had gone on long enough, so he revealed the fact that he had her diary. He confirmed that the motive for killing Badrou and Miloud was revenge. Amira could no longer hold back the tears as she hissed, "Badrou, that dirty bastard, deserved to die a thousand times."

"And Miloud Sabri?"

"Hoopoe deserved what he got."

Gradually, she began to release her buried emotions stemming from the killing of her brother, Redouane, and the shame and oppression her family endured as a result. Her mother's diabetes and high blood pressure, and how she died of grief and sorrow for her son. She saw her mother melt away like a candle. She tried the impossible to save her but failed. Her precious mother went with her wounds. Revenge was the only way to deliver a fair punishment.

"Who was your accomplice in the killing of Miloud Sabri and Badrou Bouzar?"

"I didn't have any accomplices."

Soltani realized that the interrogation had reached an impasse, so there was no point in asking more questions. He wanted to obtain a full confession and learn the name of the accomplice, but you can't always get what you want. He informed the secretary that she was being placed under arrest. She requested time to get dressed and implored him to make the arrest discreetly, to avoid a scandal with the neighbors.

The Colonel headed to General Belkacemi's office on Soummam Boulevard. He found the door open, and the General was on the phone. He signaled for Soltani to sit down, so he did. Soltani could tell by the General's features, the tone of his voice, and his carefully chosen words that he was speaking with someone from "higher up." When the call ended, the Boss took a deep breath. He then proceeded to read in a raised voice from a page in front of him, imitating a television newscaster:

> This just in from the Algerian News Agency:
>
> The great freedom fighter, Miloud Sabri, went to God's mercy this evening after having suffered a heart attack. The Ministry of Veterans' Affairs mourned the deceased with a statement that said: "With tearful eyes and humbled hearts, we mourn on behalf of the great Algerian people, our outstanding veteran brother Miloud Sabri, who gave everything he had to our beloved Algeria during the glorious Revolution and contributed to building Algeria after independence. The heart of the great freedom fighter stopped beating on Independence Day. Did his heart beat during his life for anything other than Algeria? God Almighty says: 'Among the believers are men who were true to their covenant with God; some of them have fulfilled their vow by death, and some are still awaiting, and they have not changed in the least.' Almighty God has spoken the truth. The deceased passed away and left Algeria in safe hands. Hadj Miloud Sabri will be buried tomorrow in the Martyrs and Veterans' Square in Aïn Al-Baida Cemetery. May God have mercy on the deceased, and may he rest in peace and inspire his family and his veteran brothers with patience and solace. 'Verily we belong to God, and to Him we return.' "

The Boss cast the Colonel a look of relief and said, "Thank God, we're done with the Hoopoe problem."

"How? I don't understand."

"Meaning the case is closed. Do you understand now, Soltani?"

"Does this also mean murder without consequences, sir?"

"Who told you Miloud Sabri was murdered?" asked the General, smiling.

"And Badrou Bouzar and Youssef Misbah both died accidently as well?"

"That's right."

"A car crash, for example."

"Good idea."

"Why not?! How about choking on a fish bone lodged in the throat at a lunch or dinner banquet, sir?"

"Nice. The main thing is that news of their deaths will be delayed a little bit."

"What do we do with the ones we have in custody: Driss Talbi, Abbas Badi, Nabil Talbi, Rachid Kadri and his daughter, and Amira Derbal?"

"All of them have been released."

"Don't you want to know who Amira and Nabil's accomplice was?"

"I told you, the case is closed, and if you want my frank opinion, this is a family matter."

"It's a case of fratricide, and we have no right getting involved. Is that it, sir?"

"Call it whatever you want, but we need to think of Algeria's interests before anything else, Soltani."

The Colonel was forced to listen to the Boss's nationalistic speech. He considered Algeria's reputation above all else, including justice. If the public here and abroad learned of the details of this case, doubts, suspicions, and rumors would run rampant.

"If the truth creates a scandal, then we don't need it. Algeria needs peace, stability, and a good reputation. Do you understand, Soltani?"

The Colonel preferred not to answer. He knew the Boss was trying to provoke him. He was looking for a victim onto whom he could empty his anger and avenge the insults of the higher-ups. Soltani was determined not to give him this opportunity, but he could not allow him to have the last word.

"By the way, how's Tariq doing?"

"What Tariq are you talking about, Soltani?"

"Your son, sir."

"He's well. Why do you ask?"

"Just making sure he's okay."

General Belkacemi looked at him and tried to decipher the hidden message. Soltani left without another word.

He headed home. The road was practically empty. Oran at night is a completely different city. You feel as if it is resting from the day's hubbub, happy on its own. He called his lover. The phone rang, and his heart started to pound.

"What do you want?"

"Oh, Meryouma, may God guide you, may God guide you. Which heart loves you, loves you . . . ?" Soltani sang.

"Have you eaten dinner yet?"

"No, I'm dying of hunger."

"Oh, you poor thing! Come over, and I'll warm up some dinner for you."

"I'm on my way, my love."

20

Summer 2018

Badrou Bouzar arrived at Miloud Sabri's office, a little after four, without an appointment. He was certain the news he had obtained was invaluable and would prove his superiority over his deceitful rivals, Nabil Talbi and Youssef Misbah. Badrou sat up straight and said, "We have a big problem, Uncle Miloud."

"What is it, Badrou?"

"Rachid Kadri . . . he's declared war."

"On who?"

"On you, Uncle Miloud."

Badrou realized from the way Hoopoe was looking at him that he had hit the target, as if he were saying: Who would dare declare war on me? Badrou preferred not to go too far in testing Hoopoe's patience, for the game of suspense has its rules, and the most important one was not to prolong things. He informed him that Rachid Kadri had signed a contract to publish a book of caricatures of the well-known character Brother Bandit. He also learned that he would include an introduction where he would reveal many details and secrets, the most important of which was that the caricature and Hoopoe were one and the same. He also mentioned that the publisher had the support of a well-connected businessman, and would publish the book, accompanied by a massive media campaign.

"This is scandalous, Uncle Miloud."

"No, it's a conspiracy."

"What should we do?"

"Let me think about it."

As soon as Badrou left the office, Hoopoe called Youssef Misbah, who was in the capital, and told him all about it. His brother-in-law did not hide his worry about the consequences because the publisher was just following orders. He would never risk such a thing if he did not have support from elsewhere.

"Rachid Kadri's book is a declaration of a proxy war."

"We must be prepared to confront it, Brother Youssef."

One evening, it occurred to Dolores to take a detour and stop by her husband's office after the monthly meeting at the charitable organization she ran, which provided aid to orphans. The meeting didn't run as long as it usually did; meetings sometimes ran late into the night. That night, they finished early, not because there were not enough topics on the agenda but rather because Madame Housayna, who always talked for hours on end, was not there. When Dolores was about to knock on the door, she heard Miloud's screaming voice. She leaned in closer to hear what was going on and confirmed that he was talking or arguing with Badrou. Usually, he could control his temper. What was wrong with him? She listened to their conversation and got an idea of what they were talking about. Rachid Kadri was going to publish a book of caricatures with the goal of exposing Miloud. He had assigned her brother, Youssef, to solve the problem, but all attempts to settle were in vain. Despite all promises and threats, the publisher's determination to publish the book remained unwavering.

"Rachid Kadri should have died."

"It's unfortunate that Redouane only completed half the mission, Uncle Miloud."

"He was supposed to kill Rachid *and* Souad. My orders were clear. We need to make sure now that that dog, Rachid, dies before he makes a laughingstock out of me."

"You're right, Uncle Miloud."

Dolores was overcome with horror, nearly fainting at the realization that Souad, her precious daughter, had not been killed by terrorists as she had thought. She pulled herself together so as not to fall to the floor and cause a ruckus. Silently, she retraced her steps, got in her car, and took off in no specific direction.

Dolores did not sleep that night. She lay next to Hoopoe, who quickly fell asleep, and spent hours looking at him. Who was this creature she had married and whose daughters she had given birth to? How had he deceived her all these years? How did she accept all of his responses without question? Why did she stop *asking* questions? Why did she never doubt him? He had wanted to get rid of

Rachid Kadri at all costs and was not ready to forgive Souad for running away with him. He had sentenced her to death and did everything he could to carry it out.

Dolores swore that Hoopoe would never sleep with her again. She could not touch the body of her daughter's killer. To justify her sudden change, she came up with a story, for Hoopoe was a shrewd and careful observer and didn't miss a thing.

The following morning, while they were eating breakfast, she told him, "Souad visited me in a dream."

"I hope everything's okay."

"She said she saw your grave next to mine."

"Our lives are in God's hands."

"I feel that death is close."

She started to cry, and by the look on his face, she could see how much that affected him. She guessed that the ruse was starting to work and continued to play her role until the next steps could be put into place.

When Hoopoe returned home that evening, he was surprised to find that his wife was now wearing a hijab. She tried to put a stop to his questioning and told him she had decided that from now on, she would devote her time to the hereafter. She would pray more and fast more so that God would forgive her and the rest of them. Then she expressed her desire to sleep alone, if only temporarily, in the room next to theirs. Hoopoe made a show of agreeing begrudgingly, but the truth of the matter was that he was happy with the suggestion, so he could hide his involuntary urination problem from her. In fact, Dolores had known about that for a while but did not want to embarrass him by bringing it up.

Hoopoe told his wife that he wanted to set his mind at ease concerning her health, so he took her to see a well-known doctor who combined medicine and psychoanalysis. She was not opposed. In fact, she welcomed the idea, thanked him for taking the initiative, and actually went to the doctor.

Hoopoe called the doctor two days later to inquire about his wife's health and was reassured that her condition was normal. There was no need to worry. For this reason, he was completely against giving her any medication because her psychological and physical state did not require it. Hoopoe thanked the doctor and thought about the hijab that had become fashionable even among the affluent, and that it was normal for someone to become more religious as they grew older. Then, he thought about life's many annoyances, the latest of which was Rachid Kadri. He had no desire for his wife to become yet another.

"If my wife wants to wear the hijab, she's free to do so. There are so many beautiful women who would like to serve me! And if she wants to pray and fast more, I've got absolutely nothing against that. As long as I'm the master of the situation and remain in control."

Amira Derbal imposed a basic condition on Badrou: Virginity was a red line. It was the sacred right of the future husband and also the only weapon at her disposal to tighten her grip on him and increase his attachment and desire for her. She knew that if he took her virginity, she would not have anything after that; he might toss her like a wet rag into the trash bin of whores, thus adding one humiliation to another. But she made up for the sweetness of intercourse with some of the things he enjoyed, such as allowing him to masturbate on her chest. He bought her a beautiful apartment in Saint-Eugène, along with a new car, becoming completely enamored with her. She felt no fear as she was certain of his love. What she *did* fear was Hoopoe and his daughter, Mona, Badrou's wife. They could ruin her plan for revenge.

One day they were eating lunch and discussing their relationship and how it might develop according to the rules of Islam when Badrou said, "Hoopoe is the snake's head."

"What can we do?"

"We have a plan, Lord help us," said Badrou in a lowered voice.

"A plan?! What is it?"

"Hoopoe will fall into a trap soon, Amira, my princess."

"What trap?"

"That's a big secret, my Amira."

"Don't you trust me?"

Badrou did not hold out long in the face of her insistence and disclosed his secret: He had recently begun collaborating with an influential group to overthrow Hoopoe and inherit everything. The plot would begin with the publication of a book of caricatures that would make fun of him and tarnish the prestige attached to his name. After that, sweeping him out of the way would be easy. Amira decided to put off telling Youssef Misbah this valuable secret. She thought, "I have to think carefully before making any decisions."

Zahra Misbah, aka Dolores, went to warn Rachid Kadri about Hoopoe. She headed to the newspaper where he worked and presented herself as his aunt, claiming that she was looking for him but could not find him. They gave her his cell phone number, and she called him several times, but he did not answer. Then she demanded his address. She went to his apartment in November 1st Square and rang the doorbell. When Rachid Kadri opened the door, he didn't know who she was, so she blurted out, "I'm Zahra, Rachid… Zahra Misbah."

He looked confused, so she added, "I'm Souad's mother…."

Rachid did not say a word. Baffled, he let her in and sat her in the living room. There, Zahra saw pictures of her dead daughter adorning the walls. Tears welled up in her eyes. She wanted to keep the visit short, so she got right to the heart of the matter.

"You're innocent, Rachid. You bear no responsibility for the spilling of Souad's blood. Miloud is the one who ordered the murder of my precious daughter."

Then she provided other details. She begged him to be careful because Hoopoe had decided to get rid of him the first chance he got. Just then, they heard someone open the door, and Rachid looked troubled. A young woman came in, and when she got closer, their eyes met. Dolores screamed, "Souad! Souad!" Then she fainted.

When she came to, she found herself in the arms of the beautiful young woman who said to her in a warm and gentle voice, "I'm Zuhour, Grandma... I'm Zuhour, Souad's daughter."

Dolores heard two strange stories: the story of Souad and the story of Abbas Badi. She stayed there for two hours, embracing Zuhour and crying. Before saying goodbye, she warned Rachid and her granddaughter about Miloud.

"Hoopoe is an evil man, and he will not stay silent when his reputation is at stake. He will never allow his enemies to tarnish his name."

The following day, Zuhour took a plane to Tamanrasset and rushed to tell Abbas the details of her meeting with her grandmother. He listened intently but did not say a word.

Zuhour broke the silence and said enthusiastically, "You two should meet as soon as possible."

"..."

"Shall I arrange it?"

"..."

"What do you think, Dad?"

He responded in a sad, choked voice.

"It's too late, my girl."

"No, life isn't over yet."

"My life with your grandmother ended in 1962, and the dead do not come back to life."

Zuhour's enthusiasm began to fade, and she said reproachfully, "You're always telling me about courage, but here you are running away..."

Agitated, he cut her off: "I will never allow her to see me like this with my nose cut off, alive... or dead."

The silence that followed was heavy.

Zuhour approached and hugged him as she broke into sobs. Abbas's eyes glistened with tears as he whispered in her ear, "God will reunite me with your grandmother in the life to come."

Youssef Misbah visited Hoopoe in his office to tell him something that would shake him to his core. Youssef opened an envelope and removed a stack of photographs. Hoopoe glanced at them and smiled, thinking his brother-in-law was presenting him with a beautiful young woman for his enjoyment.

"Who's this bitch, Brother Youssef?"

"If I were you, I wouldn't call her that."

"What does this bitch have that the others don't?" Hoopoe asked, laughing.

"She's your granddaughter."

"What are you saying, Youssef?"

"Souad and Rachid's daughter."

"Are you sure?!"

"Yes, very sure."

Sparks of anger flew from his eyes, and he started to yell, "Impossible! Impossible!"

Youssef did all he could to try to calm him down. Then they discussed the matter at length. They concluded that, should the story get out, it would essentially destroy the family's reputation. They had to deal with it quickly and in complete secrecy. After a short silence, Hoopoe looked at his brother-in-law and said, "I'll erase the shame with my own hand and do away with that dog Rachid Kadri and his bastard daughter."

"There's something else."

"What a horrible day! Give me what you've got, Brother Youssef."

"Abbas Badi is alive and well."

"Alive? Are you sure?"

"Very sure. He's the one who raised your granddaughter."

"My granddaughter! Are you trying to rile me up? I don't have grandchildren, do you understand?" yelled Hoopoe, furious.

"I understand. Please calm down. He gave the girl his name."

"The conspiracy is bigger than I imagined, Brother Youssef."

Hoopoe became Dolores's obsession. She watched him up close and spied on him every chance she had. The day before Independence Day, her brother, Youssef, visited them in the morning, which was not when he usually came. Soon, Hoopoe was alone with him in his office on the ground floor, and he closed the door. The windows were open, which made it easy for Dolores to listen in on them from the garden. She heard their conversation and learned that Hoopoe had decided to kill Rachid Kadri and her granddaughter the following day, on Independence Day. Dolores realized that the time had come to carry out her plan.

21

Thursday, July 5, 2018

11:25 P.M.

Colonel Karim Soltani was driving to his lover's house, enjoying the nighttime view of the sea while trying to reassure himself that everything was fine and not to overthink it. In a few minutes, he would be in Meryouma's arms, enjoying a delightful night. Who was better off than he was? The next day was a holiday, a chance for him to make it up to his son, Malik, for forgetting to take him to see his friend in Mostaganem. Despite that, he was unable to relax; he was upset. A sentence stuck to him like a tenacious, hungry fly: "Spilling the blood of traitors is halal, permissible!"

Suddenly, he turned around and hit the accelerator to head back to where he had been that morning.

The Colonel got to Canastel in ten minutes. He rang the villa's bell, and the toothless guard who had been so rude to him before opened the door. He acted differently this time, welcoming him in. The Colonel told him that he wanted to speak with Madame Dolores about an urgent matter. He took out his cell phone and made a call. After a few seconds, the guard accompanied him to the villa's interior gate. When they got there, he found the servant who had taken him to the living room. Dolores was waiting for him without a hijab. She was dressed in a green djellaba, sipping some coffee, and smoking a cigarette. She looked at him with a sad smile on her lips, remaining silent as she awaited his next move. There was no use in prolonging things.

"Pardon me, madame. I came to inform you that we have closed the investigation."

"I know." She pointed to the paper from the Algerian News Agency lying on the table.

"May God have mercy on him."

"I'm not so sure of that."

"Why not, madame?"

"You know well what he did."

"I know a little."

"What matters most is that we can rest a little easier now that Hoopoe is gone."

"Spilling the blood of traitors is permissible."

"You understood everything, sir."

"I want to hear the whole story from you, madame."

"What's the use of knowing the details now?"

"I don't like stories with loose ends."

"I'm really very tired and don't have the strength for another interrogation."

"I promise you I won't ask a single thing, madame."

Dolores finally began to speak in order to dispel any questions. She did not betray any regret or emotion.

"I decided to take revenge on Hoopoe when I discovered that it was he who ordered my daughter Souad's murder.

"Years ago, I stumbled upon a valuable secret that was of great help to me. One night, I saw Miloud, that horrible man, sneak out of the bedroom like a thief after thinking I was asleep. This awakened my curiosity, and I followed him. He left the house in his pajamas, so I ran to the window to spy on him. I saw him walking quickly, carrying a flashlight and a spade, and as soon as he reached the large orange tree in the garden, he began to dig. After a while, he removed a box, sat on the ground, opened it, and began leafing through its contents. After he finished, he put the box back where it had been and covered it with dirt. As he returned to the house, I hurried back to bed and pretended I was asleep. Miloud was very attached to the big orange tree and prevented the gardener and the guard from getting close to it. He used to say that it reminded him of the tyranny of the French colonialists; his father was crippled after falling from that tree. This is how I discovered where he hid his files.

"My chance came two weeks ago when he traveled to Madrid to have some tests done on his knees. I chose an appropriate time at night when no one was in the garden. I took a flashlight and a spade and rushed to where I saw Miloud remove the box. I dug until I found a rectangular metal container. When I lifted it out, it wasn't too heavy, so I carried it to my office to carefully examine the contents. As soon as I closed the door behind me, I opened the box, and my eyes fell on a black leather sack. I opened it and found a dagger smeared with bloody fingerprints inside a plastic bag that had 'Badrou Bouzar' written on it. And in the same box, I found three cards that were ready to send. Written on them was: 'One of you is next.' This was definitive proof that Hoopoe was the one who had been sending threatening postcards to the three of us—me, Driss Talbi, and Miloud himself—since 1962. This was the first time I suspected he was the one who had betrayed Yazid and Abbas Badi. But then I found an old file with French police stamps from the war. I opened it and found old pictures of my sister, Farida, and my brother, Youssef. Then I looked through the documents and found something horrifying: Farida and Youssef were spies, and they were the ones who had betrayed Yazid.

"I sought out someone to join me in getting rid of Miloud and succeeded in finding Nabil Talbi and Amira Derbal. I was extremely troubled after finding out that Nabil was my husband's biological son. I had to inform Nabil of the truth. It was my only chance to keep him away from Mona. How could he possibly marry her if he knew she was his sister?! He might have been thinking of marrying her out of a desire to inherit Hoopoe's fortune because Mona was his only heir. I decided to face the problem head-on. I sent him an anonymous email signed 'The Dove' with the DNA results attached. After that, I went out and spoke with him directly. Nabil's reaction was surprising. He told me a secret he had been keeping since he was ten years old: Miloud and Youssef had killed his mother, Farida, and he hoped to take revenge on them.

“Once I was sure Nabil was with me, I thought of Amira Derbal, Badrou’s secretary. Discovering that Miloud was behind the murder of my daughter, Souad, was not the only discovery. I also learned the name of the perpetrator of the crime, Redouane Derbal. After some careful investigation, I discovered that this Redouane was Amira’s brother. I didn’t know of a stronger motive for murder than revenge, so I called Amira Derbal and asked if I could see her. We agreed to meet in the Aïn Al-Baida Cemetery. I arrived half an hour before her to have a look around, and memories of the revolution and guerrilla operations came back to me. At first, she didn’t recognize me wearing a hijab; it seems the hijab completely changes how a woman looks. We sat far from where anyone could see us. I didn’t want to prolong the suspense. I noticed she was extremely nervous, so I tried to reassure her that I was uninterested in her relationship with Badrou. I explained my philosophy of life to her in simple words: Married men are like little children; they always need new things to play with. Marital boredom is a dangerous illness that must be dealt with wisely, patiently, and forgivingly. Yes, forgivingly. Amira couldn’t believe what she was hearing. I added that I don’t see losses as long as everybody benefits. And where are the victims? There are no victims. She benefits, as does Mona.

“ ‘Ah, Mona . . . Who could handle her? She’s my daughter, and I know her well.’

“Then I added that Badrou had every right to relax and enjoy himself a little. The important thing was to remain discreet and not cause a scandal. Some of the tension left Amira's face, and she was heartened.

"'What would you like me to do, madame?'

"'I have information about your brother, Redouane.'

"'Redouane?'

"'Redouane is the one who killed my daughter, Souad, may God have mercy on her.'

"'And Hoopoe and Badrou killed Redouane.'

"She surprised me when she cried and told me she had seen Miloud and Badrou killing her brother. That's how we confirmed that Redouane was the one who carried out Souad's murder, but Miloud and Badrou were the ones who planned everything out.

"At the end of our meeting, I said to her, 'Hoopoe and Badrou need to pay for this.'

"'I'm with you, madame.'

"On the other front, it wasn't difficult for Amira to trap Hoopoe. I was her advisor, as a wife naturally knows her husband's secrets inside and out. However, she didn't seem to need my advice or guidance. She was manipulating Badrou quite as she liked, and Amira seized the opportunity during one of Hoopoe's visits to Badrou's office. When he was set to leave, she accompanied him to the elevator and got in with him. When they were alone, she blinked and turned so he could look at her behind. She felt his hand on her waist. She turned back to him, smiling, and he whispered in her ear, 'You're my bitch, Amira.'

"'Yes, I'm your bitch, sir.'

"He laughed, and she laughed with him. She had passed the test, or rather, *he* had passed. Hoopoe visited

Badrou's office a lot, and every time, she accompanied him to the elevator, play-fighting with him a little bit to excite him even more. Hoopoe looked for various ways to enjoy her but only received hugs and some furtive kisses. All the while, his lust and desire for her increased.

"Yesterday afternoon, I heard Hoopoe talking on the phone in his office in a honeyed voice. I knew that the caller was Amira, who was giving him the good news that it was the night he had been waiting so long for. She would grant him her precious virginity to ring in Independence Day, to seal their partnership. He came out of his office, his eyes glistening with joy. He told me he wasn't going to eat dinner at home. I was able to get the address of the Mistress's Villa ahead of time, and made a copy of the keys. I told Driss, Abbas, Rachid, and Zuhour all about it.

"Last night, I was in constant contact with Amira, who kept me abreast of what was going on by text message. When it started to get dark, Nabil brought me in his car to the neighborhood where the Mistress's Villa was. He parked on a nearby street, and I walked the rest of the way. I entered the villa without anyone knowing. The guard wasn't there as he had taken a sick day. I hid myself in one of the rooms and waited for Hoopoe and Amira to arrive. It was a long night, during which I thought about all the major events of my life. I heard them come in and realized that my mission was about to begin.

"Amira opened the door for me. She was dressed exactly as I was—a black tracksuit and a gray cap. She played her role perfectly. Amira closed the door behind me. I stood there by myself looking at Hoopoe, hands and legs bound like an Eid sheep, writhing in despair, anger, and defeat.

"'Hello, Miloud... my life partner.'

"He froze as if paralyzed. He knew my voice.

"'The time has come for you to pay, you traitor... liar!'

"I sat on the edge of the bed. I took off my cap, and a look of fear replaced the astonishment on his face. I wore gloves. I put my hand into my small bag and pulled out the dagger I had taken from his secret box. Signs of extreme terror appeared in his eyes. I held my left hand tightly to his neck and cut the tip of his nose off. As the blood flowed, I said, 'Spilling the blood of traitors is halal, permissible. This is for Abbas Badi.'

"Miloud looked in the mirror on the ceiling and saw his face covered in blood. Then he passed out, which made things easier for me. I slit his throat from ear to ear.

"I got up from the blood-covered bed and put the dagger underneath the pillow. I took off the plastic gloves, put them into my handbag, and walked out. Amira was waiting for me outside the room.

"'Hoopoe has paid the price.'

"'And Badrou will pay the price by my hand, madame.'

"We left the Mistress's Villa together and walked to the end of the road, where Nabil was waiting for us. We got in his car and took Amira to her apartment; then I came back here. I was exhausted but felt relaxed with how the mission had gone. The guard was not there as I had sent him on a night errand to Tlemcen. I didn't need to remind Nabil of his similar mission of getting rid of that traitor, Youssef. Ah, despicable Youssef! When he learned of

Miloud's murder, he approached, anxious, asking me where Miloud hid his files, but I pretended that I knew nothing. God's curses on him and on all traitors!

"I took a hot shower to get rid of the blood and the rotten smell and told myself that killing him was the last guerrilla operation I would undertake: for my granddaughter Zuhour, for my daughter Souad, for poor Abbas. Then I remembered that it was July fifth... the first Independence Day without Miloud Sabri... without Hoopoe."

Dolores stopped talking. She took a Marlboro out of the box and handed another to the Colonel, who accepted it with a smile.

"That's the story, son," she uttered as she lit the cigarette.

"Spilling the blood of traitors is halal, Madame Dolores."

"Everywhere and always."

"Thank you, and goodbye, Madame Dolores."

"May God protect you, my son."

Soltani left the villa after saying goodbye to the guard. Before he started his car, he called his lover.

"Where are you? The food's cold, Colonel!"

"I'll be there in ten minutes. Ah... I almost forgot something important."

"What?"

"I love you, Meryouma... I love you madly."

"You're a big liar, sir."

AUTHOR'S ACKNOWLEDGMENTS

I want to express my gratitude to the friends who assisted me in writing and revising this novel: Salvatore Allocca, Mahmoud Belhimer, Sadek Benkada, Khaled Bensaleh, Aziz Bouzidi, Laurence Caillieret, Massimo Carlotto, Wasim Dahmash, Mohamed Daoud, Mariagrazia De Luca, Alexander Elinson, Belal Fadl, Judith Gurewich, M'hand Ismail, Saïd Khatibi, Francesco Leggio, Christine Love, Stephanie Love, Cherif Meribai, Kouider Metayer, Hadj Miliani, Elaine and Mokhtar Mokhtefi, Khaled al Nassiry, Lotfi Nia, and Mohamed Sari.

ABOUT THE AUTHOR

Amara Lakhous was born in Algeria in 1970 and lived in Italy for eighteen years before moving to the United States in 2014. A bilingual novelist in Arabic and Italian, he is the author of *Clash of Civilizations Over an Elevator in Piazza Vittorio*, a bestseller translated into ten languages and adapted into a film in 2010. He is currently a professor in the practice in the Department of Italian Studies at Yale University.

ABOUT THE TRANSLATOR

Alexander E. Elinson is Professor of Arabic and head of the Arabic program at Hunter College of the City University of New York. His translations include Youssef Fadel's *A Beautiful White Cat Walks with Me* and *A Shimmering Red Fish Swims with Me*, Yassin Adnan's *Hot Maroc*, Khadija Marouazi's *History of Ash*, and Saïd Khatibi's *The End of the Sahara*.